Read 2010

"Where are your folks?"
Adam Mackenzie asked the twin boys standing in front of him.

"We don't talk to strangers," they replied.

"Well, this stranger wants to let your parents know what mischief you were up to."

A screen door slammed, reverberating through the quiet Oklahoma afternoon. Adam knew he was in big trouble. She stomped toward him, brown hair lifting in the breeze. Faded jeans and a T-shirt, her face devoid of makeup and he was suddenly sixteen again.

He let out a breath and remembered why he was here. And he remembered to be angry about his car and everything else that was out of his control.

"What's going on here?" She came to a stop behind the boys.

"Your dog was in the road, and the boys were close to getting run over."

"I'm really sorry about that." She gathered her sons close, in a tight-knit huddle.

"It's okay. I just wouldn't want them to get hurt."

"You're right, of course. I'm Jenna Cameron." She held out a small hand. "Welcome to Dawson."

Books by Brenda Minton

Love Inspired

Trusting Him
His Little Cowgirl
A Cowboy's Heart
The Cowboy Next Door
Rekindled Hearts
Jenna's Cowboy Hero

BRENDA MINTON

started creating stories to entertain herself during hour-long rides on the school bus. In high school she wrote romance novels to entertain her friends. The dream grew and so did her aspirations to become an author. She started with notebooks, handwritten manuscripts and characters that refused to go away until their stories were told. Eventually she put away the pen and paper and got down to business with the computer. The journey took a few years, with some encouragement and rejection along the way—as well as a lot of stubbornness on her part. In 2006, her dream to write for the Steeple Hill Love Inspired line came true.

Brenda lives in the rural Ozarks with her husband, three kids and an abundance of cats and dogs. She enjoys a chaotic life that she wouldn't trade for anything—except, on occasion, a beach house in Texas. You can stop by and visit at her Web site, www.brendaminton.net.

Jenna's Cowboy Hero
Brenda Minton

Steeple Hill®

Published by Steeple Hill Books™

If you purchased this book without a cover you should be aware
that this book is stolen property. It was reported as "unsold and
destroyed" to the publisher, and neither the author nor the
publisher has received any payment for this "stripped book."

STEEPLE HILL BOOKS

**Steeple
Hill**®

Recycling programs
for this product may
not exist in your area.

ISBN-13: 978-0-373-87569-6

JENNA'S COWBOY HERO

Copyright © 2009 by Brenda Minton

All rights reserved. Except for use in any review, the reproduction
or utilization of this work in whole or in part in any form by any
electronic, mechanical or other means, now known or hereafter
invented, including xerography, photocopying and recording, or in
any information storage or retrieval system, is forbidden without
the written permission of the editorial office, Steeple Hill Books,
233 Broadway, New York, NY 10279 U.S.A.

This is a work of fiction. Names, characters, places and incidents are
either the product of the author's imagination or are used fictitiously, and
any resemblance to actual persons, living or dead, business establishments,
events or locales is entirely coincidental.

This edition published by arrangement with Steeple Hill Books.

® and TM are trademarks of Steeple Hill Books, used under license.
Trademarks indicated with ® are registered in the United States Patent
and Trademark Office, the Canadian Trade Marks Office and in other
countries.

www.SteepleHill.com

Printed in U.S.A.

In his heart a man plans his course,
but the Lord determines his steps.
—*Proverbs* 16:9

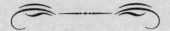

This book is dedicated to all of the people who keep climbing mountains and to those who want to climb mountains.

To my family for putting up with me.

To my friends who keep answering the phone. (Haven't you learned your lesson?)

To Janet and Melissa, for the continued support and encouragement.

Chapter One

"What do you mean, there's no money in the account?" Adam Mackenzie shouted into his cell phone.

His manager, Will, sighed from five hundred miles away. "The money is gone, Adam. Fortunately, a lot of the work on the camp has already been done."

Adam gripped the steering wheel a little tighter and went through the list of reasons why this wasn't the worst thing that could have happened to him. He had been through worse things.

The most important thing to remember: the camp wouldn't be his problem for very long. But how could the money be gone? He'd given his cousin Billy more than enough to build the camp.

"What happened to the money?" Adam leaned and flicked his gaze to the left, looking for a road that he was starting to question the existence of. Not one Internet map had directions for Camp Hope on the outskirts of Dawson, Oklahoma, population fifty.

For the last few miles, since he'd left the main highway, he'd seen nothing but fields of grazing cattle, a few small oil wells, and a smattering of aging farmhouses.

Will cleared his throat, the way he did when he didn't want to give the answer.

"What do you mean, what happened?" Will said, avoiding the answer. Adam came close to smiling, because he knew his agent that well, and he liked him that much.

"You know what I mean." Adam slowed when something moved into the road a short distance ahead. "Where did my money go?"

"It looks like Billy took a few trips, bought a car for his girlfriend and lost a big chunk of cash in Vegas." Will paused at the end of the list. "I really am sorry about this."

"It was my money." Adam wanted to yell but he didn't—this time. It wouldn't do any good to lose his temper. But it sure would have felt good.

He'd learned from experience that giving in to what feels good can get a person into a lot of trouble. He'd learned from the experience of losing contracts, being pushed off on other teams and having his face on tabloids. He'd learned that he didn't have a lot of real friends.

"I know it was your money. And now it's your camp," Will said with conviction and probably a smile, judging by his tone.

"I get that. But no way is this *my* camp, or *my* problem. I'm trying to rebuild my reputation so that the Sports Network sees the new me, not the old me, when I interview for the sportscaster job. That's my problem, Will. The last thing I need is the responsibility of a camp and a bunch of kids."

"Sorry, Adam, the camp is now your problem."

"Of course it is."

Billy had lied. Like so many other people had lied. People liked to use him. Adam's family used him. Women used him. Billy had used him.

He reminded himself of one important fact. Will, his manager for the last few years, had never used him. He had never lied.

"What am I going to do with this place?" Adam asked as he reached to flip the visor and block the setting Oklahoma sun.

Before Will could answer, something at the side of the road caught Adam's attention. A dog. *Don't move, dog. Don't make this day worse.* Worse happened to be two kids holding the leash attached to the dog. Two small boys wearing shorts, and T-shirts. Adam honked the horn. The dog looked up, but continued to back into the road, away from the boys who stood in the ditch.

"This can't be happening. Gotta go, Will." He slammed on the brakes.

The car veered and Adam held tightly to the wheel, trying to see where the kids had disappeared to. The car spun and then jolted, slinging him to the side as it came to rest against a tree with a thud.

His brand-new car. The thought barely registered when he heard the whoosh of the air bags. Other words slipped through his mind. And he still didn't know if he'd hit those kids or their dog.

His phone rang. He pushed at the air bag and freed himself from his seat belt. The phone rang again. Will's ring tone. Adam lifted it to his ear as he leaned against the headrest, waiting for his heart to stop hammering against his chest.

"I'm fine, Will."

"Do I need to call 911 for you?"

"Like I could give directions to this place. Talk about…"

"No such thing as Godforsaken, buddy."

Adam groaned as he pushed past the pain in his

shoulder. "Save the sermon for my funeral. I have to make sure these kids are okay."

"Kids?"

"There were two kids out here. I swerved to keep from hitting them and their dog."

He pushed at his driver's side door. It wouldn't open. Will was still on the other end, asking questions.

"I can't get out of my car."

"I can call for help." Will sounded a little too amused. "Doesn't that car have one of those fancy talking computers that asks if you need assistance?"

"I had it disconnected. I don't need a bossy female asking me if I'm lost or need assistance. I'll call you later."

He pushed and then kicked the passenger's side door. It opened and he climbed out of the car, stumbling as his feet hit the ditch. Thorns from a wild rosebush caught his arms and sleeves. He untangled himself and waded through tall weeds to reach the road.

The boys were standing at the edge of a gravel drive. The dog, a black-and-white border collie, sat next to them, tongue hanging out and ears perked. They watched him, eyes big and feet moving nervously— like they were getting ready to run for their lives.

He probably looked like a giant coming up out of that ditch. Especially to two little boys.

"What are you boys doing by the road?" He glanced up the drive to the old farmhouse not two hundred feet away. The house was old, but remodeled, the white siding wasn't green with moss, and the windows gleamed.

The boys shifted in front of him, tugging on the dog's leash, keeping it close to their side.

"Our dog needs to learn to walk on a leash," the heftier of the two boys, obviously twins, answered. They weren't identical, but they were close.

"Well, that dog won't do you any good if you get her hit, or get yourselves hit." He spoke as softly as he could, but it still came out in a growl. They had scared ten years off his life.

He stood at the edge of the road, thinking he should march them up to the house and let the parents know what they'd been up to.

Or he could leave and forget it all.

A glance over his shoulder and he knew he wouldn't be driving away, not in the car that was lodged against a tree, two tires flat.

He'd had some bad days of late. This one took the cake. He didn't even like cake.

"Our dog's a him," the bigger boy muttered, his gray eyes wide, not looking away. "Are you a giant?"

"No, I'm not a giant. Where are your folks?" Adam eyed the smaller boy, the one with the thumb in his mouth. The kid was shaking. Adam took a deep breath and lowered his voice. "And what are your names?"

The bigger twin started to answer. The little one nudged his brother with a bony elbow that prompted him to say, "We don't talk to strangers."

Both boys nodded and the bigger twin chewed on his bottom lip, obviously wanting to break the no-talking-to-strangers rule. Adam wanted to laugh, and that took him by surprise.

"Well, this stranger wants to let your parents know what you were up to."

A screen door slammed, reverberating through the quiet of an Oklahoma afternoon. He glanced toward the house and knew he was in big, big trouble, because he didn't have the skills for dealing with mad wet hens. She came off the front porch and stomped toward him, brown hair with streaks of blond, bouncing, lifting in the soft breeze. Faded jeans and a T-shirt, her face devoid of makeup, and he was suddenly sixteen again.

He let out a breath and remembered who he was and why he was here. And he remembered to be angry about his car and everything else that was out of his control.

"What's going on here?" She came to a stop behind the boys, her accent an Oklahoma drawl, half Southern belle and half redneck woman. She was pretty, but looked like a scrapper, like she wouldn't be afraid to come at him if he messed with her or the boys.

And the dog was growling now.

"Your dog was in the road, and the boys were pretty d—"

She raised a hand and her eyes flashed fire. "Watch it."

"Your boys were close to getting run over, and you're worried about my language?"

"Yes, sir, I am."

"Great, total insanity."

"Only partial." She smiled. Huge brown eyes lit with golden flecks caught and held his gaze. She took a few more careful steps and he realized that she wasn't much bigger than her two boys. Five feet nothing, and he felt like a giant towering over her.

Adam stamped down the desire to ask her name. He pushed aside old habits that had gotten him into more trouble than he could handle. More gossip than real trouble, but to the world, it might as well be true.

"I'm really sorry about the boys, and the dog." She had rounded up all three and they gathered close, in a tight-knit huddle at the side of the road.

"It's okay. I just wouldn't want them to get hurt."

"You're right, of course. I'm Jenna Cameron." She held out a small hand with pink-painted nails. "Welcome to Dawson."

"Yeah, thank you. I'm looking for a half-finished summer camp."

"You sound happy about that."

"Real happy." Because he never expected to lose his cousin, and he hadn't expected the camp to be unfinished. He pulled the directions out of his pocket and read them off to her. "Do you have any idea where that is?"

She stepped to the edge of the road and pointed. Three hundred feet ahead, on the other side of the road and barely visible due to shrubs and grass, was a gravel drive. "That's your place."

"You've got to be kidding." He took a step closer to her and the dog snarled, raising an upper lip in a pretty convincing warning. Adam backed away.

"Sorry, he's my guard dog." Her hand rested on the dog's head. "I'm afraid I don't reprimand him for doing his job."

"No need, as long as he doesn't bite me." He didn't want to add dog bite to the things that had gone wrong today. He looked at the overgrown drive and the address on the crumpled paper in his hand. "Are you sure that's it?"

It was a cow pasture dotted with trees. He couldn't see much of the property because trees lined the fence row that ran parallel to the road.

"That's it. Earlier this summer they were working up there, until…well, anyway, they built a barn and a dorm. They even hauled in a single-wide mobile home."

"At least he did that."

"So, *you're* the owner."

"I'm the lucky guy." He shoved the paper back into his pocket and walked back to his car. She followed, slower, taking it easy over the rocks. The boys and the dog remained at the edge of the road, all three looking at him like he might be public enemy number one.

He was used to that look, more used to the look than to kids. He had made a careful choice not to date women with kids. Or at least he'd had that policy since Morgan.

"You're probably going to need help getting your car out of that ditch." She walked closer, eyeing the car. She smelled like soap and peaches, not Chanel.

"I don't think this car is going anywhere anytime soon."

"I can give you the number of the local garage," she offered, looking up at him. "They can tow it for you."

"Are you going to pay the tow bill, seeing as it was your kids who caused the wreck?"

"If you insist."

"No, I don't insist. Forget it." He glanced back at the boys and the dog. "They're cute."

"Thank you, Mr. Mackenzie, and I really am sorry." She bit down on her bottom lip and averted her gaze back to his car.

He didn't know what to say. She knew him, which meant that even here he couldn't find anonymity. And it wouldn't be long before his family knew that he was back in Oklahoma.

Jenna looked away from the pale blue eyes of the man towering over her. She'd get a crick in her neck if she kept looking up at the six-and-a-half-foot giant, whom she knew well from watching football with the guys in her unit. His face was all smooth planes beneath a sandy-brown goatee, and when he smiled, there was something about it that changed his eyes, making her think a light was hiding inside his heart. It was a kind of shy smile, almost humble, but powerful.

Maybe it wasn't real. It could be a part of his lady-killer image. As an optimist she liked to think that it was something else. It was the real person hiding inside the public image, hidden by tabloid stories of models and actresses.

She'd like to know the real Big Mac Mackenzie.

But of course, she wouldn't. Getting to know a man wasn't on her five-year plan. Or her fifteen-year plan. She would get her boys and walk back up the drive to her house, away from the temptation to ask him questions about his life and why he was here now.

He had finished checking out the wrecked car and walked back to her, shaking his head.

"Is it bad?" She was mentally calculating what a car like that would cost, and how much the repairs would cost her.

"No, I don't think so. Two tires are blown, and there's a good dent in the driver's side door."

"Do you want the number for the garage?"

"I guess I have to." He pulled a cell phone out of his pocket.

"Sorry, you'll have to come up to the house for the number." Jenna gathered the boys and looked back over her shoulder.

He was standing in the road, looking unsure, like this was all some malicious trap on her part. He looked like a giant, but he looked lost and a little vulnerable. She shook off the thought that compared him with David, her smallest twin, after he'd had a bad dream.

Big Mac Mackenzie wasn't a lost child. He was a grown man standing in the road wearing faded jeans, a loose white shirt with the top three buttons undone and a black cowboy hat firmly in place.

"Are you coming?" She waited. "I'll get you a Band-Aid for the cut on your head."

He finally nodded, let out a sigh and took long-legged strides that soon put him next to them. And then he walked slower, keeping pace with them as they made their way up the drive to the house.

Horses whinnied from the barn, reminding Jenna that it was feeding time. She glanced in that direction, thinking of work that needed to be done, and how she'd rather be sitting on the front porch with her leg up and a glass of iced tea on the table next to her.

She loved her front porch with the ivy and clematis vines climbing the posts, drawing in bees and butterflies. She loved the scent of wild roses in the spring. Like now, caught on the breeze, the scent was sweet and brought back memories.

Some good, some bad.

"What are your names?" Adam Mackenzie asked the boys, his deep voice a little scary. Jenna gave a light squeeze to their hands to encourage them.

"Timmy." The bigger of her two boys, always a little more curious, a little more brave, spoke first. "And we don't talk to strangers."

He also liked to mimic.

"Timmy, mind your manners," Jenna warned, smiling down at him.

"Of course you don't, and that's good." Adam Mackenzie turned his attention to the smaller of her two boys. "And what about you, cowboy?"

"I'm David." He didn't suck his thumb. Instead he pulled his left hand free from hers and shoved his hands into his pockets. He looked up at the tall, giant of a man walking next to him. "And we have a big uncle named Clint."

A baritone chuckle and Adam made eye contact with Jenna. She smiled, because that light was in his eyes. It hadn't been a trick of the camera, or her imagination. She had to explain what David had meant to be a threatening comment about her brother. Leave it to the boys to think they all needed to be protected from a stranger.

"My brother lives down the road a piece."

"Clint Cameron?" Adam's gaze drifted away from her to the ramp at the side of the porch. Her brother had put the ramp in before she came home from the hospital last fall.

"Yes, Clint Cameron. You know him?"

"We played against each other back in high school. What's he doing now?"

"Raising bucking bulls with his wife. They travel a lot."

Jenna grabbed the handrail and walked up the steps, her boys and Adam Mackenzie a few steps behind, watching her. The boys knew the reason for her slow, cautious climb. She imagined Adam wondering at her odd approach to steps. In the six months since she'd been home, she'd grown used to people wondering and to questioning looks. Now it was more about her, and about raising the boys. She was too busy with life to worry about what other people were thinking about her.

It hadn't always been that way. Times past, she worried a lot about what people thought.

She opened the front door, and he reached and pushed it back, holding it for them to enter. She slid past him, the boys in front of her.

"Do you want tea?" She glanced over her shoulder as she crossed the living room, seeing all of the things that could make him ask questions about her life. If he looked.

He stood inside her tiny living room in the house she'd grown up in. A house that used to have more bad memories than good. For her boys the bad memories would be replaced with those of a happy childhood with a mom who loved them.

There wouldn't be memories of a dad. She wasn't sorry about that, but then again, sometimes she was.

The walls of the house were no longer paneled. Clint had hung drywall, they'd painted the room pale shell and the woodwork was white now, not the dark brown of her childhood. The old furniture was gone, replaced by something summery and plaid. Gauzy white curtains covered the floor-to-ceiling windows, fluttering in the summer breeze that drifted through the house.

Everything old, everything that held a bad memory, had been taken out, replaced. And yet the memories still returned, of her father drunk, of his rage, and sometimes him in the chair, sleeping the day away.

Adam took up space in the small house, nearly overwhelming it, and her, with his presence. As she waited for his answer to the question about iced tea, he took off his hat and brushed a hand through short but shaggy sandy-brown hair.

"Tea?" He raised a brow and she remembered her question.

"Yes, iced tea."

"Please. And the phone book?"

"The number for the garage is on my fridge." She led him down the hall to the kitchen with a wood table in the center of the room.

She loved the room, not just the colors—the pale yellow walls and white cabinets. She loved that her sister-in-law, Willow, had decorated and remodeled it as a way to welcome Jenna home. The room was a homecoming present and a symbol of new beginnings. They had worked on the rest of the house as Jenna recovered.

Jenna poured their tea while Adam dialed the phone. When she turned, he was leaning against the wall, watching her. She set the tea down on the table while he finished his conversation.

"Is it taken care of?" She pulled a first-aid kit from the cabinet over the stove.

"They'll be out in an hour. They wanted to call the police to write up an accident report."

Jenna swallowed and waited for him to tell her how he'd responded to that. Accident. She hadn't really thought about that. Her boys had caused an accident. She pulled out the chair and sat down, stretching her legs.

"I'm so sorry. You really could have been hurt."

"Your boys could have been hurt."

She nodded. "I know. The rule is that they don't go down the drive. They're usually very good boys."

"I'm sure they are." He picked up the glass of tea. "I'm going to need to rent a car."

"Not around here. And I want to finish talking about the accident report. You'll need to let them call the county so you can get this covered on your insurance."

He drained half the glass of tea in one gulp and set it down on the table. "I'll take care of it."

"Just like that, you'll take care of it?" She bit down on her bottom lip, waiting, because it couldn't be this easy. "My boys caused an accident and major damage to an expensive car."

"They didn't really cause the accident. I saw their dog backing into the road...."

"And that caused the wreck. They were holding the leash of the dog that backed into the road."

"Wow, do you plan on making this difficult?"

"No, I'm just trying to do the right thing."

"You can give me a ride down to that Godfor—"

She lifted her hand and shook her head to stop him. "Watch your language."

He shook his head. "Great, another Will."

"Excuse me?"

"My manager, Will. Did he hire you to keep me in line?"

"Sorry, no, you're a big boy and you'll have to keep yourself in line. Now let me put a Band-Aid on your cheek. You're bleeding." She motioned to the chair as she stood up and opened the first-aid kit. "Sit."

"I'm fine."

"I can't have you get an infected cut on my watch."

The boys hurried into the room. They must have heard her mention that he was injured. They were wide-eyed and impressed as they stared at the cut.

"It's gonna need stitches," Timmy informed their victim, peering up, studying the wound.

"Do you think so?" Adam asked, reaching to touch the cut.

"Don't touch it, just sit." Jenna pointed again to the chair.

He sat down at the kitchen table, giving her easier access to his face. His eyes were closed and when she touched his cheek he flinched.

"That hurts. What are you putting on it, alcohol?" He pulled away from her fingers.

Her fingers stilled over the small cut and he opened his eyes, looking at her. She glanced away. "I'm cleaning it. It doesn't hurt that bad."

He looked at the boys. Jenna glanced over her shoulder and smiled at them. They were cringing, twin looks of angst on their suntanned faces.

"It's really bad," David whispered.

"Does it need stitches?" Adam asked them, not her. As if they were the authority.

The boys were nodding. "It has a lot of blood."

Timmy and David stepped closer.

She shook her head. "Don't listen to them. It won't even leave a scar."

She pulled the backing off the Band-Aid with fingers that trembled as she put the adhesive strip in place. She felt like a silly teenager watching the star football player from across the dining room of the local Dairy Bar. She'd never been the girl that those football players dated.

"Finished?" He touched his cheek and pushed the chair back from the table.

"Finished. Now, if you want, I'll drive you to the camp."

"That sounds good. I'll make a call to the rental company and have a car delivered."

Settled, just like that.

With Adam "Big Mac" Mackenzie behind her, she walked out the back door. As she headed for her truck, she walked slowly, hoping he wouldn't notice if she stumbled.

But what did it matter? She was who she was. And Adam Mackenzie was passing through.

The boys were climbing into the backseat of her truck squabbling over who sat on what side. She smiled, because that's who she was, she was Timmy and David's mom. But as she opened her truck door, she caught Adam Mackenzie's smile and she was hit hard by the reality that she was more than a mom. She was obviously still a woman.

Chapter Two

Adam slid into the old truck and slammed the door twice before it latched. He glanced sideways and Jenna Cameron smiled at him, her dimples splitting her cheeks and adding to her country-girl charm. He knew a dozen guys that would fall for a smile like that.

He knew he'd almost fallen when he looked up as she dabbed salve on his face and caught her staring with brown eyes as warm as a summer day. She'd bitten down on her lower lip and pretended she wasn't staring.

The boys were buckled in the backseat of the extended-cab truck. They were fighting over a toy they'd found on the floorboard. He wondered where their dad was, or if they had one. Jenna Cameron: her maiden name, so she wasn't married. Not that he planned on calling her. He had long passed the age of summer romances.

The truck, the farm, a country girl and two little boys. This life was as far removed from Adam's life as fast food was from the restaurants he normally patronized. He kicked aside those same fast-food wrappers in the floor of the truck to make room for his feet. A toy rattled out of one of the bags and he reached to pick it up.

"This should stop the fighting." He reached into the back and the boys stared, eyes wide, both afraid to take the plastic toy. "I'm not going to bite you."

They didn't look convinced. Jenna smiled back at them. He would have behaved, too, if that smile had been aimed at him. The smaller twin took the toy from his hand. Another look from Jenna and the boy whispered a frightened, "Thank you."

The truck rattled down the drive and the dog ran alongside. When they stopped at the end of the drive, the dog jumped in the back. What would his friends think of this? And Morgan—the woman he'd dated last, with her inch-long nails and hair so stiff a guy couldn't run his fingers through it—what would she say?

Not that he really cared. They'd only had three dates, and then he'd lost her phone number. How serious could he have been?

"You grew up not far from here, right?" Jenna shifted and the truck slowed for the drive to his *camp*. He couldn't help but think the word with a touch of sarcasm. It was the same sarcasm he typically used when he spoke of *home*.

"Yeah, sure."

"Are you staying with family?"

"Nope." He rolled his window down a little farther. He wasn't staying with family, and he didn't plan on talking about them.

He'd taken his father into the spotlight he craved, and now it was over. Retirement at thirty-three, and his father no longer had the tail of a star to grasp hold of. They hadn't talked since Adam announced his retirement.

Over the years his relationship with his family had crumbled, because they'd made it all about his career. His sister had faded away a long time ago, probably before high school ended. She'd yelled at him about being a star, and she wasn't revolving around his world anymore. And she hadn't.

The truck bounced over the rutted trail of a drive that had once been covered with gravel. Now the rain had washed away the gravel and left deep veins that were nearly ditches. The truck bumped and jarred. Overgrown weeds and brush hit the side panel and a coyote, startled by their presence, ran off into the field. The dog in the back of the truck barked.

"This can't be the place."

"Sorry, it is." Jenna flashed him a sweet smile that didn't help him to feel better about the property, but he smiled back.

She reminded him of girls who'd wanted to wear his letter jacket back in high school. The kind that slipped a finger through a guy's belt loop as they walked down the hall and kissed him silly on a Saturday night.

"If it makes you feel better, there are plenty of people around here looking for work." She broke into the silence, speaking over the wind rushing through the cab of the truck and country music on the radio. "Take a drive into town and there are half a dozen guys who will mow this with a Brush Hog."

"That's good to know." Not really.

He sighed as they continued on. Ahead he could see a two-story building with rows of windows. Probably the dorm. To the left of the dorm was a stable, and to the right of the dorm, a large metal-sided building. Jenna parked in front of a long, single-wide mobile home.

"Home sweet home." She pushed the door open and jumped out. "It really is a good quality mobile home. And there's a tornado shelter."

She pointed to a concrete-and-metal fixture sticking up from the ground. A tornado shelter. So, the manager would duck into safety while fifty kids huddled in a dorm. He didn't like that idea at all. Billy probably hadn't given it a second thought.

Billy had lived a pretty sketchy life for the most part. A few years ago he'd found religion and then a desire to do something for troubled kids. Adam had thought Billy's plan for the camp was legit. Maybe it had started out that way.

Adam walked toward the mobile home, wading through grass that was knee-high. The boys were out of the truck and running around, not fazed by grass or the thought of snakes and ticks.

He would have done the same thing at their age. Now, he was a long way from his childhood, not far from home, and the distance had never been greater.

"Do you know a Realtor?" He looked down, and Jenna Cameron shook her head.

"Drive into Grove and pick one. I couldn't tell you the best one for the job, but there are several."

His cell phone rang. He smiled an apology and walked away from her, leaving her looking toward the stable with a gleam that was undeniable. Most women loved diamonds, not barns.

"Are you there?" Will's voice, always calm. That's what he got paid for. Will was the voice of reason. Will prayed for him.

Adam had bristled when Will first told him that a few months back. Now the knowledge had settled and he sometimes thought about why his manager would think he needed prayer.

"If this is it, I'm here. And I'm…"

"Watch it, Adam." Will's endless warning.

"Fine, I'm here. It's paradise. Two hundred acres of overgrown brush, a drive with more ruts and ditches than you can imagine and my living quarters are a trailer."

"It could be worse."

"So you always say. Is that a verse in the Bible? I can't remember."

Will laughed. "Close. The verse says more about not worrying about today's troubles, tomorrow's are sufficient in themselves."

"Is that supposed to make me feel better? Can't you think of something more optimistic?"

"Has it been so long since you've been to church?"

"Your kid's dedication when she was born."

"She has a name."

"Yeah, she does. Kate, right?"

"You're close. It's Kaitlin."

"See, I'm not so shallow and self-centered."

"I never thought you were. So, about the camp…"

"I'm going to contact a Realtor."

"No, you're not. Adam, you can't ditch that place."

Adam glanced in the direction of the cowgirl and her two kids. They were tossing a stick for the dog and she was pretending not to listen. He could tell she was.

"Why am I not selling?" He lowered his voice and turned away.

"Because you need this patch on your reputation. You need to stay and see this through. You need to be the good guy."

"My reputation isn't bad enough for this to be the punishment."

"Look, Adam, let's not beat around the bush. You have money in your account, a nice house in Atlanta and a shot at being a national anchor for one of the biggest sports networks in the world. Don't mess it up."

Adam walked up the steps to the covered porch on the front of the mobile home. He peeked in the front door, impressed by the interior and the leather furniture his cousin had bought with his money.

"Adam?"

"What do you want me to do?"

"Is this compliance?" Will sounded far too amused and then he chuckled, as if to prove it. "Stay there. Clean the place up and make it a camp for underprivileged kids. Show the world what a good guy you are."

"I'm not a good guy, I'm self-centered and macho. I'm a ladies' man. I worked hard on that reputation and now you want me to change it?"

"I didn't ask for the other reputation, it's the one you showed up with. This is what I'm asking for. That you stay for the summer, show the world the real you, and be nice to the neighbor."

Adam glanced in her direction, blue jeans and a T-shirt, two little boys. "How do you know about her?"

"Billy told me she's a sweet girl."

"You talked to Billy?"

"He called to ask a few questions, just advice on the property."

"I don't like this. You do realize, don't you, that I'll have to live in this trailer and eat at a diner in Dawson called The Mad Cow?"

Will laughed and Adam smiled, but he had no intentions of staying here. He'd find a way to get out of it. He pushed his hat down on his head and walked off the porch, still holding the phone.

"Billy said the chicken-fried steak was to die for." Will the optimist.

"Billy died of a heart attack. Talk to you later."

* * *

Jenna picked her way across the overgrown lawn. Adam Mackenzie stood next to the porch, staring at the barn and the dorm. He looked a little lost and kind of angry. Angry didn't bother her. Neither did tantrums—she had the twins.

"Bad news?" She stopped next to him and looked up, studying his face.

"Nothing I can't handle." He tore off a piece of fescue grass and stuck it between his teeth. "My agent thinks I should stay. This sure wasn't where I wanted to spend my summer."

"Really?" She looked out at land that, with a little care, could be a premium piece of property. And she thought of the kids, the ones who were so much like herself, who could come here for a week or two and forget the abuse or poverty at home. Couldn't he see that? "It looks like a great place to me."

"What do you see that I don't?"

"Promise. I see kids finding a little hope and maybe the promise of a better future. I see kids escaping for a week and just being kids."

He groaned and tossed the grass aside. "Another optimist."

"I call it faith."

"So does Will." Adam had turned back to the steps that led up the porch. "But how does faith help me solve this problem? Does faith clean this place up, or finish it so that it can be used?"

"Prayer might be the place to start."

"Right."

She followed him up the steps, right leg always first. It was getting easier every day. Ten months ago she had wondered if anything would ever be easy again. Adam turned when he reached the top and gave her a questioning look she ignored.

"I'm sorry, it really isn't my business." She answered his question, pretending the look was about that, about him wanting an answer. "I just happen to believe that God can get us out of some amazingly bad situations."

"Well let's see if God can help us get into this trailer."

She watched as he shoved a credit card into the door. The boys were in the yard playing with the dog. "Guys, stay right here in front of the trailer. Snakes are probably thick right now."

"That's another positive." He pushed the door open and stepped inside. Jenna followed.

He looked around, focusing on the phone and answering machine. Jenna waited by the front door, not sure what she should do. Maybe she should go home? Maybe now was the time to remove herself from his presence and this situation.

While she considered her options, he pressed the button on the answering machine. Messages played, mostly personal and a little embarrassing to overhear knowing that Billy was gone and this was his legacy. There were messages from a distraught girlfriend, creditors asking for money, and his mom wondering why he didn't call.

Adam replayed the last message.

"Billy, this is John at the Christian Mission. I wanted to confirm that we have the third week of June reserved for fifty kids. Can you give me a call back?" The caller left a number.

Adam turned. "What's today?"

"The sixth of June."

He groaned and tossed his hat on a nearby table. "I can't believe this."

The message replayed and he scribbled the number on a piece of paper.

"What are you going to do?" Jenna sat down on a bar stool at the kitchen counter.

"Cancel this camp."

"And let those kids down?"

"I didn't let them down, Billy did. I can't have someone bring fifty kids to this place."

"But…" She bit down on her bottom lip and told herself it wasn't her business. Not the camp, not his life, none of it. She was just the mom of the kids who ran him off the road.

"Fifty kids," he repeated, like she didn't get it. "I don't even know if the buildings are finished."

He sat down on the stool next to hers and it creaked. "Obviously the bar stools aren't one size fits all. Look, I'm not a bad guy, but this isn't my thing. Summer camps, Oklahoma, none of this is me."

"I know you're not a bad guy. And you're right, this isn't my business. You have to make the decision that's right for you."

He smiled, and she liked that smile, the one that crinkled at the corners of his eyes. "You're slick, but you're not going to work me this way."

"I wasn't trying."

"Of course not." And his smile disappeared.

"I would help you." She hesitated, at once sorry, but not. "I mean, it wouldn't take much to get the camp ready."

"Don't you work?"

"I have two boys and ten horses. That's my work. But with the help of the community…"

She hopped down from the stool, momentarily forgetting, and she stumbled. A strong arm caught her, holding her firm until she gathered herself. Her back to him, she closed her eyes and drew in a deep breath.

"Are you okay?" He stood next to her, his hand still on her arm. Looking up, she realized that his face was close to hers, his mouth a gentle line.

"Of course I am."

He laughed, the deep baritone filling the emptiness of the dark and shadowy trailer. "Of course you are. You waited a whole five minutes after meeting me to involve yourself in every area of my life, and I can't get a straight answer on if you're okay. I know a knee injury when I see one. Remember, I've spent a lot of years getting plowed over and pushed down."

"It's an old injury." She smiled but it wasn't easy in the face of his unexpected tenderness, the baritone of his voice soft, matching the look in his eyes. "I need to check on the boys."

He released her. "And I need to check on the barn and the dorms to see how much more money I'm going to have to spend to make this place usable."

"But I thought you weren't going to run the camp."

"I'm not running it. I'm going to get it ready for someone else to run. I'll let you and my noble agent, Will, run it. Or I'll put it up for sale."

Jenna grabbed a tablet off the counter and the pen he had tossed down. "We'll drive down there. I can help you make a list for what you might need."

Because she didn't feel like making the long walk through the brush on the overgrown trail that used to be a road. The boys were sitting on the porch steps, holding a turtle they'd found.

"Can we keep it?" Timmy poked at the turtle's head.

"No," she answered as she walked down the steps of the porch.

"Why not?" all three guys asked.

"Because it wouldn't be happy in a box. It belongs here, where it can travel and find the food it likes, not the food we toss to it every day."

The boys frowned at the turtle and then at Jenna. "We just want to keep it for a little while."

David touched the back of the box turtle, fingers rubbing the rough shell. "I like him."

Adam sighed and walked back into the house. He came back with a permanent marker. "Guys, there is a way you can keep an eye on this bad boy. We'll write your names and today's date on the bottom of his shell. When you're out here, you can find him and see how he's doing."

And that's how he became a hero to her boys. Jenna watched, a little happy and a lot threatened. She couldn't let Adam into their lives this way.

Herself in his life, that was different. Making sure this place became a camp was important to her. It was important to kids who were living the same nightmare childhood she had lived.

It was about the camp, not about Adam "Big Mac" Mackenzie. She honestly didn't need to understand his smile, or the way his eyes lit up. It had been easy, imagining his story when he'd been a football player she and the guys cheered for. Now, with him so close and his story unfolding, she didn't want to know more.

Adam climbed back into the truck. The boys piled in with them this time because it was a short ride across a bumpy drive to the barn. He glanced sideways, catching a glimpse of Jenna Cameron with her sun-streaked brown hair windblown and soft.

He wasn't staying. He wouldn't be pushed into this

by her, or by Will. They'd have to understand that he was the last person in the world who ought to be running a camp, dealing with children, especially in Oklahoma.

As soon as he could figure out what to do with this place, who to turn it over to, he'd head back to Atlanta, back to his life. Back to what?

He sighed and she flicked her gaze from the road to him. That look took him back more than a dozen years, to pickup trucks and fishing holes, summer sun beating down on a group of kids just having a good time.

There hadn't been many times like that in his childhood. His dad had always been pushing, always forcing him onto the practice field. He had sneaked a few moments for himself, enough to make a handful of memories that didn't include football.

And she brought back those memories, most of which he had forgotten.

The truck stopped in front of the barn. She shot him a questioning look. "It needs a corral."

He nodded, like he knew. A long time ago he would have noticed. The barn sat on an open lot, no fences, no arena, no corral.

"It's probably going to need more than that."

"Horses wouldn't hurt." She smiled and then reached for the door handle to get out of the truck.

He followed her, walking behind her into the shadowy interior of the barn. One side was a stable. The other side was for hay, equipment and a room for tack. It creaked in the Oklahoma wind.

She looked up, questions in her brown eyes. The boys shrieked and she glanced in their direction. They were outside, the dog next to them barking.

"Timmy, David, what are you doing?"

"Snake!" the two shrieked at the same time. And

Adam noticed that they didn't scream in fear, but in obvious boyhood delight.

"Get them." She looked up at him, expecting him to be the one to run to the rescue of her offspring. And he didn't think they wanted to be rescued. "Please, Adam."

She couldn't run to them, and she wanted to. He could see it in the tight line of pain around her mouth. Ignoring the fact that the running he wanted to do was in the direction of Atlanta, he ran to the end of the stable and gathered the boys in his arms, pulling them back from the coiled snake. A garter snake, nonpoisonous and no threat to the boys or the dog.

"It's a garter."

The boys wiggled to get free. He set them down, knowing that they'd go back to the snake. The reptile slithered along the side of the barn now, in search of a warm place to rest. The dog had lost interest and was sniffing a new trail.

Jenna was leaning against the barn, watching them, a soft and maternal smile turning her lips.

"Come on, guys. I think you've caused enough commotion for one day." She motioned them to her side. "Mr. Mackenzie, don't give up on the camp. I know someone would buy it, live here, raise some cows. But a camp. Not just everyone can do that."

"Probably true, but I'm not the person who can."

"But you have to." She turned a little pink. "I'm sorry, you don't have to."

He wanted to smile. He wanted to ask how a person became so passionate about something, so willing to fight for it.

"Why does it mean so much to you?" As the words slipped out, he thought he probably didn't want the answer.

"It isn't about me. Not really. I think you shouldn't

give up on something that could mean so much to so many people. Including you. And, believe it or not, I think it meant a lot to Billy."

"But it doesn't mean that much to me. I'm not looking for good deeds to do. This was about my cousin, something he wanted to do, and something that I had the money to help him with."

"If you didn't believe in this when Billy proposed it to you, why did you give him the money?"

"I don't know." And he didn't. He looked out the open doors of the barn and fought the truth. Maybe he did know why. Maybe he hadn't run as far from his roots as he'd thought.

"It's too bad that it won't be a camp. Come on, boys, we're going home. It was nice to meet you, Mr. Mackenzie." She said it like she was disappointed in him, as if she had expected better from him. But she didn't know him.

Before he could say anything, she was walking away, the boys running a little ahead of her. The dog went in another direction, chasing a scent that interested him more than the direction his family was going.

As she climbed into her truck, not looking in his direction, he felt strangely let down. A thought that took him by surprise. She wanted this camp, not for herself but for the kids it could help.

At least it meant something to her. To him, it was just another way he'd been used.

He headed back down the driveway, toward the road, because the tow truck would arrive soon and the rental car he had ordered would be delivered in an hour.

The Mad Cow Diner was starting to sound pretty good, another sign that he was nearing the end of his rope. The lifeline he had to hold on to was the reality that he could take care of what needed to be done, hand it off to someone else, and leave.

Jenna Cameron's truck rattled down the rutted driveway, slowing as she reached the road, and then pulling onto the paved road in the direction of her house.

Chapter Three

"What's up with you?" Vera sat down at the table across from Jenna. The Mad Cow wasn't crowded in the afternoon and the boys were enjoying slurping up chocolate shakes.

Jenna had fallen into a stupor. The black-and-white, Holstein-spotted walls of the diner had become a little hypnotic as she'd sat there, her elbow on the black tabletop, her chin on her hand.

Vera, dark hair pulled back in a bun and a smock apron over her white T-shirt, filled Jenna's cup and set the coffeepot down on the table.

Jenna picked up the sugar container and poured a spoonful or more into her coffee. "Why do you think something is up?"

Vera smiled as if she knew everything that was going on, and even what might happen. "Oh, honey, we all know that Adam Mackenzie crashed into your ditch the other day."

"It wasn't my ditch." She stirred creamer into her coffee. "It was the ditch across from me."

"He came in for my chicken-fried steak last night, and the night before."

And that made him Vera's hero. He would be Jenna's hero if he kept Camp Hope alive. That didn't seem too likely. Besides, she didn't need a hero. She had two little boys who were slurping up the last of their shakes and eyeing someone else's French fries.

"I think those boys need fries." Vera slid out of her chair. "Don't despair, Jenna dear. It'll all work out."

"I know it will, but I really want that camp."

Vera's brows went up in a comical arch. "*You* want it?"

"For kids. Can you imagine what a treat that would be for children who don't normally get to attend camp?"

Kids like her, when she was ten or twelve, and broken, feeling like no one cared and God was a myth, meant only to keep naughty children on the straight and narrow.

She'd had a hard time with *straight and narrow*.

"I can imagine." Vera's hand rested on her shoulder. "Give it time. I don't think he'll ditch it. If he isn't going to run it, someone else will."

But would someone else run it at no cost for the kids attending, the way Adam's cousin had planned? She wished she had the money to buy it. But wishes were vapor and her bank account was barely in the black.

"Mom, how does a person get to be a football player on TV?"

Timmy's question shook her from her thoughts. She smiled at him. His lips were back on his straw and Vera had left, pushing through the doors, back into the kitchen.

"Lots and lots of work," she answered, and then pulled the cup away from him and pushed the small glass of water close. "The shake is gone, drink some water."

"Vera's making us some fries." He grinned, dimples making it even cuter, even harder to resist. "She whispered that it's 'cause we're the best boys she knows. She's putting cheese on them, the way we like."

He added the last with a lilt of an accent that was meant to sound like Vera. Jenna kissed his cheek. "You're the best boys I know, too. And we might as well order burgers, since you won't want supper now."

David's eyes lit up. He pushed away the empty shake glass and sat down in the chair that he'd been perched on, sitting on his knees to better reach his glass.

"Do you think I could be a pro football player some-day? I'd make a lot of money and you could have a big house in, well, somewhere." Timmy was out of his chair, standing next to it. He didn't like to sit still, a reality that had caused problems in school last year.

First grade was going to be rough for him, a whole day of sitting still, listening.

"I don't need a big house and you should only play football if you love it, not because you think I want a big house." She didn't think Adam Mackenzie loved the sport. She wondered if he ever had.

She had asked Clint, because her brother had known Adam years ago. Clint said he really couldn't say. Adam had seemed intent, serious, but he didn't know if he had loved it.

Vera returned with their fries. "What else, kiddos?"

"Go ahead and bring us three burgers, Vera. We'll let you cook for us tonight."

Vera was all smiles. "You got it, sweetie. Three Vera specials coming up."

The door opened, letting in heat and sounds from outside—a train in the distance and cars driving down Main Street. Vera's eyes widened. Jenna glanced back, over her shoulder and suddenly wanted to get her order to go.

* * *

"Jenna Cameron, imagine seeing you here." Adam stood next to Jenna's table, smiling at the two boys because it was easier than smiling at her, easier than waiting for an invitation to join them and easier than dealing with the reality that he wanted to join them.

He told himself it was just pure old loneliness, living at that trailer, not having his normal social life. He was starved for company, that's all.

"You knew I was here. My truck's right out front." She smiled up at him, a mischievous look in eyes that today looked more like caramel than chocolate.

He laughed. "You got me there. I thought I'd swing in for Vera's meat loaf and I wanted to tell you something."

"Have a seat." She pointed to the chair on her left.

He hesitated, but her wide eyes stared up at him, challenging him. He sat down, taking off his hat as he did. He hooked it over the back of the empty chair on the seat next to him.

The boys occupied the two chairs across the table from him. Blond hair, chocolate milk on their chins and suspicious looks in their eyes, they stared at him in something akin to wonder.

"So, what's your news?" Jenna leaned back in her chair, hands fiddling with the paper that had come off a straw.

"You get your camp."

"Excuse me?"

"I'll be staying, at least through the end of July. My agent thinks I should stay and help get the camp running." He wouldn't expand on Will's words, which had been a little harsher than what he was willing to admit to Jenna. "I called the church that left the message and told them I might be able to get something going in time, or close to it. If they can be flexible."

Her eyes widened and he could see the smile trembling at the corners of her mouth. "I can help."

"I thought you might."

Vera pushed through the swinging doors of the kitchen carrying a tray of food and avoiding eye contact with him. Probably because she'd been listening in. At least she didn't have a camera or an agenda.

Or did she have an agenda? Probably not the one he was used to. More than likely Vera had only one agenda. She had matchmaking on her mind. She had the wrong guy if that was her plan.

"Did I hear someone mention my meat loaf special?" She set down plates with burgers in front of Jenna and the boys and pulled a pen and order pad out of her pocket. "I've got that chocolate chess pie you like."

"No pie tonight. If I don't start cutting myself back, you'll have me fifty pounds overweight when I leave Dawson."

Vera's brows shifted up. "Oh, don't tell me you're still in a hurry to get out of here?"

"Not anymore. I'm going to stay and make sure things are taken care of at the camp."

Across from him the boys stopped eating their burgers and looked at each other. It was a look that settled somewhere in the pit of his stomach, like a warning siren on a stormy afternoon. Those two boys were up to more than seeing who could get the most ketchup on their fries.

At the moment David was winning. He had a pile of ketchup on top of two fries and he was moving it toward his open mouth. Adam held his breath, watching, wanting the kid to win, and maybe to break into that big grin he kept hidden away.

Just as David started to push the fry into his mouth, the front door to Vera's opened. David looked up and his fry moved, dropping the ketchup. Everyone at the table groaned, including Adam.

"That isn't the reaction I normally get when I walk into a restaurant." The man stepping inside the door was tall, a little balding and thin. The woman behind him smiled, her gaze settling on Jenna.

"No, it's usually the reaction you get when you tell one of your jokes on Sunday morning," the woman teased with a wink at Jenna, punctuating the words.

"Pastor Todd, Lori, pull up another table and join us," Jenna offered a little too quickly and Adam got it. She wasn't thrilled with the idea of Adam Mackenzie at her table. He sat back, relishing that fact.

A little.

Until it got to him that she wasn't thrilled to be sharing a table with him. Jenna cleared her throat and a foot kicked his.

"Excuse me?" He met her sparkling gaze and she nodded to Pastor Todd.

"Could you help him move that table over here, push it up against ours?"

"Oh, of course." Adam stood up. And he remembered his manners. "I'm sorry, we haven't met."

"Pastor Todd Robbins." Todd held out his hand. "My wife, and obviously better half, Lori."

"Adam Mackenzie."

And they acted like they didn't know who he was. Maybe they didn't. Not everyone watched football. He reached for the table and helped move it, pushing it into place as Jenna had directed. And Vera still watching, smiling, as if she had orchestrated it all.

"So, what first?" Jenna wiped her fingers on a paper towel she'd pulled off the role in the center of the table.

"What?" Adam looked surprised, like he'd forgotten the camp. She wasn't going to let him forget.

"The camp. You'll need beds, mattresses, food…"

He raised his hand, letting out a sigh that moved his massive shoulders. "I don't know where to start. I don't see any way this can be done in a matter of days."

"Weeks."

He didn't return her smile. "Yeah, well, my glass of optimism isn't as full as yours. We have less than two weeks. And then we have kids, lots of them, and they need activities."

"Not as many as you might think. I think if you talk to their church, they have lessons planned, chapel services, music. You need the beds, window coverings. They'll bring their own bedding." She stopped talking because he looked like a man who couldn't take much more. "Oh, horses."

She whispered the last, in case he was at the end of his rope and about to let go.

"Horses?"

"Clint can help you with that."

"Is there some way that I can help with this project?" Todd broke in. "I'd be glad to do something."

"We'll need kitchen help, and people to clean the grounds and the cabins." Jenna reached for her purse and pulled out a pen. She started to write, but Adam covered her hand with his.

She looked at his hand on hers and then up, meeting a look that asked her to stop, to let it go. He turned to Pastor Todd.

"Let's talk about it later, maybe tomorrow. Not now."

He was in denial. Poor thing. And so was Jenna if she thought she was immune to a gorgeous man. She moved the hand that was still under his, and he squeezed a little before sliding his hand away.

"Okay, tomorrow." But she was no longer as sure as she had been. Adam smiled at her, like he knew what she was thinking. So she said something different to prove him wrong. "Clint will be back tomorrow."

With that she let it go, because it hit her that she had just invited this man into her life. He was the last person she needed filling space in her world, in her days.

The horse tied in the center aisle of the barn stomped at flies and shook her head to show her displeasure with the wormer paste they'd pushed into her mouth. The tube said green apple. Jenna had no intentions of trying it, but she doubted it tasted anything like an apple. She patted the horse's golden palomino rump and walked around to her side, the injection ready with the animal's immunizations. Clint stood to the side. He and Willow had come home early and he'd surprised Jenna by showing up this morning to help with the horses.

"Why are you so quiet today?" Clint slipped the file back into the box of supplies he'd brought in. This horse's hooves hadn't needed trimming, which meant he had just stood back and watched as Jenna did what she needed to do.

And now she wished she had more to do so she could ignore his question. He knew her far too well.

"I'm not quiet."

"Yes, you are. Normally when we get home from a trip you have a million questions. 'How did Jason do this week?' He did great, by the way. Got tossed on his head."

She looked up. Leaning against the horse's back, watching from the opposite side of Clint. "Is he okay?"

Jason was one of her best friends. She sometimes

regretted that they'd never really felt anything more than friendship. He'd make a great husband for someone. He was kind, funny, wealthy. And not the guy for her.

"He's fine. And Dolly has gone ten outs without being ridden."

"That's great. I bet Willow is proud."

"She is. They're considering him for the finals at the end of the year."

"Great."

"And then we flew home in the pickup."

"I'm so glad."

"And you're not listening to me."

Jenna stared out the door at the boys, watching them play in the grassy area near the barn. The dog was sitting nearby, watching, the way he watched cattle in the field. If he had to, he'd round the boys up and drive them to her. They loved it when he did that. Sometimes they wandered away from her just to see if the dog would circle and move them back to Jenna. The nature of a cow dog was to herd. Jenna was glad she'd brought home the black-and-white border collie. It had been a cute, fluffy puppy, and was now a great dog.

"Jenna, is everything okay?"

"Of course it is. I'm just tired." She smiled back at her brother. "Let's get this horse out of here and bring Jinx in."

"Who is that?" Clint walked to the door as the low rumble of an engine and crunch of tires on gravel gave an advance warning that they had company. And then the dog barked.

Dog. She really needed to name that poor animal. It was probably too late. The boys called him Puppy and Jenna called him Dog. He came to either name so it seemed wrong to call him something like Fluffy or Blue.

"I don't know." Jenna tossed the used needle into the trash.

"Big, blue truck."

She groaned and Clint shot her a look. "You know who it is? Did you sell that roan gelding?"

"Jenna?"

"It's Adam Mackenzie." She untied the horse, rubbing her neck. "Come on, girl."

"That's it? Adam Mackenzie is pulling up to the barn and you act like you expected him?"

"He's the mystery owner of the camp."

"Adam is building a youth camp?" Clint followed her to the barn door with the mare. "The mystery deepens."

Jenna laughed. "It isn't a mystery. Billy was his cousin and he convinced Adam to buy the land and start this camp."

"Sis, you know he's trouble, right?"

"I don't think he's trouble. I think he's confused."

Clint shook his head. "Remember when you thought a baby skunk would be a good pet because it didn't spray you?"

"I remember."

She laughed at the memory. Because eventually the skunk did spray her. She gave it to a zoo and missed school for a week. She really did learn by her mistakes. Sometimes it just took a few tries before the lesson sank in.

Men were included in the list of mistakes she'd learned her lesson from. The father of her boys had walked out on her. He went back to California, and she let him go because she knew she couldn't force him to stay and love them. The soldier she'd fallen in love with, he'd written her a Dear Jane letter after her surgery.

She would never again own a pet skunk. She would

never again fall for a pretty face and perfect words. She had a five-year plan that didn't include falling in love.

"He's getting out of his truck," Clint warned as he took the halter off the mare and slapped her rump to send her back to the field with the rest of the horses.

Jenna nodded. "He wants to talk to you about buying horses. And since he's here to see you, I'm going to the house."

"Are you running?" Clint followed her to the front of the barn. And the twins were no longer sitting in the grassy area with their toy cars.

"Nope, just leaving."

"Are you afraid of him?" Clint caught hold of her arm. "Jenna, did he say something to you?"

"No, and I'm not afraid." *Much.* "I have to check on the boys. They've abandoned the road they were building for their toy trucks. I need to see where they went."

"That's because they're showing Adam something." He nodded in the direction of the blue truck that was parked a short distance from her house.

"Great." She watched the boys open their hands. Two blond-headed miniatures with sneaky grins on their faces, and dirt. They needed baths.

The giant in front of them jumped back from their open hands, either feigning fear or truly afraid. The boys laughed, belly laughs, and then they ran off.

Adam Mackenzie turned toward the barn, his smile a little frazzled. He wasn't used to kids. She had to give him points for trying. And she wasn't going to escape because he was heading their way.

Who could escape that moment when they felt as if their insides had jelled and their breath caught somewhere midway between lungs and heart?

All due to a cowboy in faded jeans and a T-shirt. Not

a cowboy, she reminded herself. A football player with a life so far removed from this small community that she couldn't imagine what it was like to live in his world.

"Adam." She greeted him with a wavering smile.

"Jenna." He held his hand out to her brother, his white hat tipped down, shading the smooth planes of his suntanned face. "Clint Cameron. I haven't seen you since we played against each other our senior year."

"Fifteen years." Clint shook Adam's hand. Jenna waited, wondering what came next. "Jenna said you're back to take care of the youth camp."

This time Adam smiled at her, that slightly boyish yet wicked grin that made his blue eyes dance. "Yeah, something like that. It looks as if I'm in charge, and I need horses. Maybe a dozen or so, with tack."

"Got it. I think I can round them up. It might take a few weeks."

"I don't have a few weeks." The edge was back in this voice.

Jenna looked up. She watched as her brother considered the words of the other man. And she made a way to escape.

"I need to get supper started. I'll let the two of you take care of business."

Chapter Four

Adam watched Jenna go, surprised that she was leaving. Let down? No, of course not. He wanted space, time out from relationships. He wasn't let down by her walking away.

He was surprised, and a little bruised by her lack of interest. Typically she was the kind of woman he ran from. The kind that was looking for a husband and a father to her kids. She didn't seem to be looking, though.

Horses. Clint's one word brought Adam back to his surroundings, and his gaze shifted back to the man standing in front of him, away from the retreating back of a cowgirl.

"A dozen, at least." He followed Clint into the barn. "She runs this place by herself?"

"She does."

"Impressive."

Clint shrugged and walked into the tack room. He hung up halters and lead ropes that were tossed on a shelf. "She's always been strong."

"It has to be tough, raising two boys alone."

"It is, but she has family and friends who help."

Adam picked up a currycomb and ran the sharp metal over his hand. "High school was a long time ago, Clint. If you're still holding a grudge about Amy, I'm sorry. I didn't know she was playing a game with the two of us."

Clint turned, smiling in a way that felt a lot like a warning snarl from a dog. "Amy is fifteen years of water under the bridge and I have no regrets. I have a wife that I love and a baby that we adopted a few months ago. My concern now is for my sister."

"You don't have to be concerned on my account. I'm here to get this camp mess cleared up, and then I'll be leaving. I'm not here looking for a relationship."

Clint shook his head and walked out of the room, switching the light off as he went, leaving Adam with just the light from outside. When he stepped out of the tack room, Clint was waiting.

"Adam, Jenna's an adult. She's also my sister. Don't use her. Don't mislead her. Don't hurt her."

"She's not a kid."

Clint took a step closer. "She's my kid sister."

Adam lifted his hands in surrender. "I don't plan on hurting your sister. I don't plan on getting involved with her at all. She's offered to help me get this camp off the ground so I can leave. Believe me, my only goal is to get this done and get out of Oklahoma."

"Okay, as long as we understand each other." Clint grabbed a box and walked out of the barn. "I'll get back to you on the horses."

"Thanks." Adam watched Clint Cameron drive away and then he turned toward the two-story farmhouse, a small square of a house with a steep, pitched roof. The boys were playing in the front yard and a sprinkler sprayed a small patch of garden. The few trees were tall and branched out, shading the house, a few branches brushing the roof.

The boys. He couldn't remember their names, and he'd had dinner with them yesterday. He walked in the direction of the house, thinking about their names, and not thinking about why he was still here. Timmy and David. He remembered as he walked up to them.

He smiled when the bigger boy looked up, a suspicious look on a dirt-smudged face and gray eyes like his uncle Clint's. The little boy, wearing shorts, T-shirt and flip-flops, sat back on his heels. He picked up his toy soldiers and nudged his other brother.

Adam knew their names, but couldn't remember which was which. "One of you is Timmy, the other is David."

"I'm David." The one who sucked his thumb. The little guy wouldn't look up.

"I'm Timmy." The bolder of the two. "And we still don't talk to strangers."

It was a long way down to the ground. Adam sighed and then he squatted. "I'm not really a stranger now. Aren't we sort of friends?"

David looked up, gray eyes curious. "Are you friends with my mom?"

"I guess."

"Did you know her in the army?" The little guy pushed his soldiers through the dirt. "Were you there?"

"No, I wasn't in the army."

He hadn't known Jenna was in the army. But did he ask little boys about their mother, and about the military? He didn't think so.

"She was in Iraq." Timmy solved the problem of Adam asking for more information.

"That's pretty amazing." More amazing than he could imagine. She wasn't much bigger than her boys, but he had pegged her right. She was tough. She had something that so many women he'd met lately didn't have. She had something…

"Boys, time to come in for supper."

She had two boys and no interest in him.

Adam stood and turned. She was standing on the porch, leaning on a cane. He didn't know what to do. Had she heard their conversation? Her face was a little pink and she avoided looking at him.

He should go. He shouldn't get involved. He didn't ask the women in his life if they were okay. He didn't worry that they looked more wounded emotionally than physically. He didn't delve into their private lives.

He had easy relationships without connecting because if he didn't connect, he didn't get used. The girl in high school, Amy, had used him against Clint. She had used them both for her own games that he still didn't understand. As much as he had lived life, he still didn't always get it. Maybe because his childhood and teen years had been spent on the football field guided by his dad, and without a lot of social interaction off the field.

"Do you want to stay for supper?" It was Timmy, holding a hand out to him, not Jenna offering the invitation.

"I should go." He looked down at the little guy and tried to remember when he'd last had supper cooked in a farmhouse and eaten at an oak table.

"You can stay." Jenna walked onto the porch, her brown hair pulled back in an unruly ponytail. "I have plenty. It's nothing fancy."

He pushed his hat back and stared up at her, a country girl in jeans and sneakers. He resented Billy for putting him in this position and Will for telling him to stay.

Because this felt like home. And he hadn't been home in a long time.

It had been so long that he'd forgotten how it felt, that it felt good here, and safe.

"Adam?"

"I shouldn't…"

"What, shouldn't eat? Are you afraid it'll ruin your boyish figure to eat fried chicken?"

"Fried chicken, you say?" His stomach growled. "I think I might have to stay."

He couldn't remember the last time he'd had fried chicken. Or the last time he'd known a woman that cooked fried chicken.

Timmy pulled his hand, leading him up the stairs. Jenna limped back into the house. He followed her slow pace, telling himself that questions weren't allowed.

He had rules about women, rules that included not asking questions, not getting personal. Because he knew how much it hurt to be used, to be fooled. But he couldn't admit that, because he was Adam Mackenzie, he could take a hit and keep going.

"What can I do?" He pulled off his hat and hung it on a nail next to the back door.

Jenna turned, her face flushed. "Pour the tea? I have glasses with ice waiting in the fridge."

"I can do that." He opened the fridge. Four glasses. She had expected him to stay. Did she think she was going to have to take care of him while he stayed in Oklahoma? He'd have to make sure she understood that he didn't need that from her.

But not today. Today there were shadows in her eyes. Today his heart felt a lot like that grassy field behind his trailer—a little empty, kind of dusty.

And Jenna Cameron looked like the person that needed to be taken care of.

He poured the tea and carried the glasses to the table. The boys were setting out the plates and flatware. He smiled down at them. They, unlike their mother, smiled back.

As Jenna came to the table with the chicken, the boys dropped into their seats. Jenna sat down, sighing like it was the biggest relief in the world to sit.

"David, pray please."

Pray? Adam watched as the boys bowed their heads. He followed their example, remembering back to his childhood and meals like this one.

The prayer was sweet, really sweet. The way only a kid can pray—from the heart. The little boy had prayed for their meal, and for soldiers and for the new baby that Willow said wouldn't let her sleep. And he prayed for Adam because he was a new neighbor.

Adam smiled at Jenna as she stood again, going for something on the counter. He should have offered. Before he could, she stumbled, catching herself on the counter.

He started to stand, but Timmy shook his head.

"Are you okay?" He scooted his chair back.

"I'm fine."

"My mom got injured in the war," David whispered. "But she's good now. We take care of each other."

A warning if ever he'd heard one.

"Maybe you need to take a few days off. I can find other help."

She put a basket of rolls on the table. "I don't need a day off, Adam. There are no days off from life."

She was one tough lady. He had to give her that. And when he left that night, he knew that she was different than anyone he'd ever met. He drove away from her house, relieved that his stay here was temporary. And he ignored the call from his sister, a call that would have required explanations.

Jenna awoke with a start, her heart hammering in her chest and perspiration beading across her forehead. It took her a minute to place this dark room—her room in the farmhouse she'd grown up in, not the dark room in Iraq that had been her hiding place. As the fear ebbed, she became more aware of the knife-sharp pain in her leg. It throbbed, and she couldn't close her eyes without remembering the sweet lady who had tried so desperately to fight the infection and save the limb.

Jenna had survived, though. Her prayers that she would live, that she would come home to her boys, had been answered. Every day she remembered those prayers and she was thankful. Even on nights when she couldn't sleep.

Fear and pain tangled inside her, both fighting to be the thing that took over, that consumed her thoughts, forcing her to focus on them, not on the good things in her life.

She could control it. She had learned ways to deal with it, even on nights like tonight when it hurt so much she didn't know if she would ever be okay again.

She closed her eyes, breathing deep, thinking about being home, and her boys, and God. The pain lessened, but her heart still ached because the dream tonight had gotten mixed in with the memory of Jeff, the last time she'd seen him. He hadn't been able to look at her.

He had sent her a letter to say goodbye.

The next day the counselor had asked her to write a five-year plan. She hadn't included love or marriage. Nor had she included them in her fifteen-year plan. Her plan included raising her boys, dedicating herself to making them young men that she could be proud of. Her plan included being at home, alive and healthy with her family. And her plan included thanking God every day for giving her a second chance at life and faith.

The list had included never having a man look at her like that again, that look that wavered between pity and horror, as if he couldn't get out the door fast enough.

The throbbing pain continued, bringing an end to the trip into the past and the return of her convictions. She reached for crutches and pulled herself out of bed. Slow, steady and quiet, she left her bedroom and eased through the house.

At the front door she stopped, looking out at what was left of the night, and watching as the eastern horizon started to glow with the early-morning light of sunrise. The trees and fields were still dark, making a perfect silhouette against the sky as it lightened into pewter and lavender.

She walked out the door, easing it closed so it didn't bang against the frame and wake the boys. Outside the air was cool, but damp with morning dew. Horses whinnied and somewhere in the distance dairy cows bellowed in the morning as they stood in line at the barn to be milked.

She hobbled down off the ramp and across the lawn, greeting the day and praying as she went. The pain faded to a less intense throb, rather than the breathtaking pain that had kept her awake.

She stopped, letting the world come into focus. Unafraid.

As she walked, the dog joined her. She reached down, petting his dark head. He froze, whining and then snarling low.

"Stop that, silly Dog." Jenna spoke with a lightness she didn't feel at the moment. Her heart picked up speed, because she heard it, too. Footsteps on the road, coming fast, much faster than she could run.

"Shhh, Dog, quiet." Jenna patted the dog's head, calming him, wishing she could calm herself as easily. The footsteps were closer. And then she spotted the figure of a man. The dog barked at the shadow standing at the end of her drive.

"Jenna?"

Adam Mackenzie. Her heart was pounding and cold chased up her arms. She froze, knowing she couldn't escape. She waited, the dog no longer snarling at her side.

"Jenna?" He called out louder. She could see him clearly now, coming up her drive.

He wore shorts and a T-shirt. She was in cutoff sweats and a T-shirt. She stared down at her foot, waiting. When she looked up, he was in front of her. His gaze lifted from the lost leg to her face.

"You're pale."

Not the first words she expected from him, but it gave her a minute to gather herself. "Because you scared the life out of me."

"What are you doing out here?" He hadn't turned away. He was still looking at her.

"The same as you, taking an early-morning run."

He looked like he didn't know if he should laugh or not. She smiled, wanting him to be the way he was yesterday, before he knew. But if she had a wish, she wished she could go back further in time than yesterday. A year, maybe more. She'd make wiser choices. She would be more careful.

But this was her reality and it couldn't be changed. Deal with it. And Adam needed to deal with it, too.

"Adam, that was a joke."

"Oh, okay."

"Please, don't do this. Don't get weird on me."

He nodded.

"I mean it." Anger put power behind her words. "Don't look at me like that."

"I'm not. You can give a guy a minute or two to adjust, right?"

"Fine, but I'm heading for the house and I'm making coffee."

"Is that an invitation?"

"Not really." She smiled up at him, glad that he was still talking, still being real. The tightness that had gripped her heart was letting go, releasing. "Yes, I guess it is."

"What are you doing out here at this time of the morning?" He walked next to her as they neared the house. "Or is that question off-limits?"

"I couldn't sleep." She stopped. "Some nights are worse than others."

"Pain?"

He opened the back door and motioned her inside.

"Yes." She flipped on the kitchen light and reached for the coffeepot. He leaned against the counter and watched. His shirt was stained dark with perspiration. She remembered jogging. Someday she'd be fitted with a limb that made it easier to run. Now, she wore one that worked for riding horses and living on a farm.

Her life hadn't ended on that summer day in Iraq. It had started over, with new obstacles, and new moments when God proved Himself. She had met Him there, in the desert, as far from church and Sunday-school lessons as a person could get.

She poured water into the coffeemaker and added fresh-ground beans, leaning on the crutches, but her hands free. She was good at this now, at balancing, at moving and continuing with everyday duties that had always seemed like second nature. Before. Her life was cut into chapters. This chapter was about learning to be the person she really wanted to be. The last chapter was the "Jenna who was whole" chapter.

But she hadn't really been whole. She had been missing something vital. Faith.

The coffee started to brew. She turned and Adam was waiting, watching her.

"What happened?" Adam pushed out a chair for her and took the one next to it. He looked like a giant at her table. A big golden-tan giant with hair that glinted in the soft overhead light.

"We were in a convoy and we were attacked." She closed her eyes as the memories came to life. "I remember being on the ground and the sand was hot and I could feel that I was bleeding. I knew the enemy was close and I didn't think I'd live to see my boys again."

"Jenna, we don't have to do this." Adam's big hand covered hers.

She looked up, and he was looking straight at her. His gaze held hers and he didn't look away. She didn't know how to feel about that, about him here in her kitchen, coffee brewing and the rooster crowing in the morning.

She smiled. "It's okay, I don't mind. I've told the story before. I have to tell people what God did for me that day."

"Oh."

Was that him discounting God, and disconnecting? "Oh?"

"I'm sorry, go ahead."

"I managed to move a short distance from where I'd been hit, but then I couldn't move any farther. I had one of those moments. You know how they say your life flashes before your eyes? Well my life hit me between the eyes. Good memories and bad came at me. I remembered stories from Sunday school. I remembered being picked up by various neighbors or by church buses and hauled to nearly every church in the county. I remembered oatmeal cookies with butterscotch chips. And I remembered those stories of Jesus. I had never really thought that He loved me enough to die on a cross for me. No one ever loved me that much, except maybe Clint. At least that's what I thought when I was eight." She looked across the room at the blurping coffeepot. "The coffee is ready."

"I'll get it, you talk." His chair scooted on the tile and she watched him pour coffee and then add sugar to hers.

"You really want to know all of this?"

"Yep."

"Okay, I'll keep talking." Because maybe that was the reason for his early-morning jog and her early-morning walk. Maybe God had brought Adam all the way to Oklahoma for this moment. "I had all of those thoughts and I thought of my boys and I knew that I couldn't die. And I knew that I could no longer deny God. After that I passed out and I don't know when I woke up again."

She took the coffee and added more sugar from the bowl on the table. His eyes widened as he watched her add the two spoons and creamer.

"Want coffee with your sugar?"

"Only a little." She sipped and it was just right.

"What happened next?"

"An elderly lady saw the attack and she sent her nephew out to rescue me before the insurgents found me. He dragged me back to their shack and they hid me. The lady had once been a nurse and she knew enough to keep me alive."

"Not enough…"

"To save my leg." Jenna sipped her coffee. Out the

window the sun peeked over the eastern horizon where the sky was streaked with pink against blue. It promised another beautiful June day with clear skies.

She couldn't look at Adam Mackenzie.

"It had to be hard for you."

"It wasn't easy," she whispered, holding the hot cup of coffee between her hands.

"Is it easy now?"

"It's getting easier all the time. I have faith, my life and my boys. I have a career training reigning quarter horses."

She didn't stop to think of the things she didn't have, and wouldn't have. Willow had told her those were self-imposed "can't haves." If that was the case, so be it. She wouldn't have a man in her life. Especially when he looked at her with pity. She wouldn't have a man in her life when she knew she couldn't let him look at her. And what man would want to look at her?

"It's that easy?" He shook his head and she smiled, because she could hear that he didn't believe it.

And she had to be honest with him. "It isn't always that easy. I get angry. I get down. I give up. And then…"

"You pick yourself up again. You would have made a great football player."

"Thank you." And she no longer wanted to talk about her. "Now do me a favor, let's talk about you. How does it feel to be home?"

"This hasn't been my home for a long time."

"Of course not. I understand that because I left as soon as I could get away. I went into the military so I could live anywhere but here. But family and roots have a way of bringing us home."

"Family and roots didn't bring me home. Unless, I guess, you consider Billy dying."

"Why haven't you gone home to see your family?"

"Because I…" He laughed. "You almost got me. All of this emotion, and you almost pulled me in."

"You're right, it was a trap. I shared my sad, pathetic little story just to get you to engage with your inner child. But there is no child in there. The tough guy squashed him."

"Exactly. And I have been home, just not in a few years."

"I hear the boys." Jenna stood, wobbling a little before she got her balance.

"That's my cue to go?"

"It is. They wouldn't understand that it's morning and…"

"I get it." He stood in front of her, towering over her. He smiled, but then the smile faded and he leaned.

Jenna choked a little and leaned back. "I don't think so, cowboy. I'm not a woman who plays games."

Adam looked startled, his head tilted to the side a little like the dog when she smacked his nose for messing with her garden or chasing the cat.

"You're right. I'm sorry." He reached for his ball cap and walked out the back door. On the step he paused. "Will you still be over later?"

"An almost kiss doesn't mean that I'm not going to help you. I'm not going to give you an excuse for backing out of helping those kids."

He nodded, and she watched as he jogged away, her dog running alongside him. She listened as the boys scuffled around upstairs, the sound of a normal day starting. But she knew that today was anything but normal.

Today Adam Mackenzie was her neighbor and she stood at the screen door, looking out at the morning, wondering what that meant to her life. Or if it meant anything at all.

Chapter Five

The Dawson Farm and Home Store was pretty close to empty at mid-morning, two hours after Adam nearly made a big mistake. Kissing Jenna would have been that, and more. He could think of a dozen reasons why.

But he didn't have time for thinking. He walked down the aisle that held horse tack and livestock vitamins, looking for what he thought he might need in the coming weeks. He hadn't bought farm supplies in a few years.

Instead of shopping for farm supplies, he should have been at home in Atlanta, preparing for a new career. Billy should be here, buying supplies, talking to locals and getting the camp ready to go. Not Adam, a guy who had spent less time with children than almost anyone he knew.

"You might want to grab mineral blocks." A familiar voice.

Adam turned from the shelf of vitamins and insect repellants. Clint Cameron stood next to him, comfortable with his life of cowboy and local hero. Adam's boots were still too new to be comfortable.

"Yeah, there's a lot to get done, a lot to buy." Including the mineral blocks, Adam realized. And if he needed them, that meant Clint had come through for him.

"I have ten horses." Clint's hat was tipped low. "I'm still looking for two more."

"That's good. Can you deliver?"

"Yeah, this afternoon if that works for you. I bought tack for them. I'll bring the bill."

"I'm sure you will."

Clint picked up a few cans of fly spray. Adam wondered if he should do the same. But if he did, he'd look like he didn't know what he was doing, like he was taking cues from Clint. And he didn't want to look like a novice. He had grown up on a farm. He knew what he needed and what he didn't.

Clint tossed him a can of the fly spray. "You'll probably need this."

"I know that." His collar felt really tight on his neck.

"Adam, we're not enemies, just guys who used to know each other and we had a few run-ins. That was a long time ago. Now we're two guys doing business, and I'm part of the community that wants to help you get this camp off the ground. Maybe you could give us all and yourself a break in the process."

"Yeah, of course." He grabbed another can of the fly spray. "I guess I'll see you this afternoon."

"Sure, at about two."

The front door chimed. Clint waved and Adam's collar felt a little tighter. Jenna, her blond-streaked brown hair pulled back in a ponytail. She smiled at her brother and then at him. Her smile for Adam was different, it was strained. He knew how she felt.

This morning he had wanted to kiss her. Good thing she'd reminded him of the boys and her desire not to get sidelined with someone like him. Good thing, because

Clint Cameron was two feet from him, giving him a look that nailed him into the floor.

She adjusted easier than he had, shifting her attention away from him, sweeping that look from her eyes that said she remembered.

"Are you two up to no good?" She had a cheeky expression and a Southern drawl.

"I'm up to good. I can't speak for your brother." Adam smiled back. How did a smile change everything?

"He's always up to good." She slipped an arm around her brother. "He's just that way. I'm the bad one in the family."

"I don't buy that."

"It's true. I'm the rebel. But I'm a rebel with a cause. We're making a schedule for when people will start showing up to work at the camp."

"I appreciate that."

She laughed. "No, you don't. You're thinking it's going to cost you."

He was, but he shook his head to deny her accusation. "Not at all."

"It's going to cost you big-time. Church, this Sunday. You need to be there and thank people, maybe tell them your plans for the camp."

"I don't really have plans." He had plans, but the plans were about his life, his future, not a camp in Dawson, Oklahoma.

"You have to have plans. Oh, and I have a catalog where you can order what you need for the dorms. Do you want me to do that?"

"This afternoon. If you want to come over, we can use my phone and get that wrapped up." How did he tell her no? She was a pint-sized dynamo, intent on her mission. He nearly smiled.

She hugged Clint and winked at Adam before turning to walk away. He watched her go, but turned when Clint Cameron cleared his throat to get his attention.

"She's my sister, Adam."

"I know she is. Don't worry, I'm just looking to get this camp taken care of so I can leave."

"This is a real inconvenience for you, isn't it?"

"It definitely isn't convenient, Clint. Look, I didn't set out to run this camp. I'm not a bad guy. I'm not unfeeling. I gave money to my cousin because he wanted to help kids who couldn't afford camp. He wanted to do something good with his new Christian life. What he did was swindle me and then he had a heart attack."

Clint smiled. "Adam, sometimes God has a plan that we can't even begin to imagine. Maybe you coming here was His plan all along."

"Right, thanks for the sermon." He walked off, leaving Clint standing in the aisle with fly sprays and vitamins. He couldn't wait to get out of a store that smelled like chemicals, dusty grain and molasses.

As he stood at the counter paying, he watched Jenna Cameron walk across the parking lot that the farm store shared with The Mad Cow.

Jenna could have imagined a thousand scenarios as she pulled up the drive to the half-finished summer camp that afternoon. She never would have imagined Adam Mackenzie on the back of the big bay that Clint had decided to sell. She eased off the gas and let her truck coast to a stop. The boys jumped up from the backseat to lean into the front and watch the man on the back of the big red horse, black tail flagging proudly as it trotted around the yard.

He looked good on a horse. A tall giant of a man, his

white cowboy hat pulled low, his jaw set as he held the reins and controlled the barely broke gelding.

The horse sidestepped, prancing and then bunny hopping as he tried to convince the man in the saddle that he might actually buck. Adam kept the reins tight and his legs visibly tightened around the animal's middle.

"Let's get out, Mom. I want to see if that mean old horse starts to buck." Timmy climbed over the seat and fell into the spot next to Jenna. David remained in the back. She glanced back at him. His eyes were wide and his mouth a firm line of seriousness.

"We're not going to get out. We don't want to spook Ready." The horse had been named *Ready, Set, Go* as a foal, because Willow thought he always looked like he was about to race.

"It might be fun to see him spooked," Timmy mumbled.

"That isn't nice."

"I don't want Adam to get hurt. I wanna see if he can stay on."

Jenna didn't laugh. Instead she hugged her son and motioned for David to climb over the seat and join them. She loved them so much. And her heart still ached when she thought about how close she came to not coming home to them. She didn't want to close her eyes, because when she did, it came back—the fear, the darkness, the thoughts of not being there to watch them grow up.

Adam reined the horse in and slid off. Jenna opened her door to get out. "Come on, guys, let's go see what we need to do around here today."

"We need to find our turtle." David slid out of the truck, already searching the grassy area around them. "We might want to feed him some bugs."

"As long as *you* don't eat bugs, that's fine," Jenna

teased, ruffling her fingers through David's blond hair as he stood next to her.

The boys looked up at her, eyes wide and twin looks of serious contemplation. Timmy held her gaze for a moment and then looked down, kicking at a clump of grass.

"Boys, we don't eat bugs." Because they really looked like they might have already tried. "Do we?"

"Not anymore." And then they ran off. She laughed and watched them go.

No more distractions. Nothing else to keep her from joining the men.

Adam was standing next to the horse, tall, making the sixteen-hand horse look small, and talking to her brother with a hint of a smile on his face. She likened him to Goliath. And she really felt as if he had come to devour her kingdom.

Of course he hadn't, though. That was just her imagination. He couldn't hurt her. He couldn't hurt the people she loved. She didn't know why she had put him in that category to begin with.

He smiled at her and pushed his hat back. "Nice horse, isn't he? Clint brought ten, and this one."

"I thought he might like something for himself," Clint explained.

"You're just looking for someone to take that grain-eating beast off your hands." Jenna rubbed the massive head of the bay gelding. "He's a pain."

"He's not. I just don't have the time to ride him the way he needs to be ridden," Clint explained, and she wanted to tell him he could have brought the horse to her. But he wouldn't do that, she knew. He didn't want her to get hurt.

"Come into the office and I'll write you a check." Adam motioned them all to the trailer that had become his residence. Jenna followed the men, their longer strides eating up the ground. She wasn't in a hurry. A summer breeze swirled through the overgrown lawn, rustling last year's leaves, and the smell of a freshly cut hayfield carried on the wind. Days like this were for enjoying, not rushing through.

Inside would be stuffy. And crowded.

The boys were playing at the corner of the trailer. They were looking for the turtle, searching the grassy area as if they'd lost a treasure. Of course it was a treasure; it was a turtle. And what boy didn't consider those a treasure?

Girls liked them, too. Jenna had had her share of box turtles as a kid. She stopped to watch the boys for a second. They talked in whispers about the turtle and Adam falling off Ready. And then they looked up and smiled, a little guilty, too cute.

Adam cleared his throat. "Are you coming inside with us?"

"Oh, sorry, I was watching the boys. They're still looking for that turtle."

"I saw him the other day. He's still around."

"I hope they find him, not another snake."

Clint laughed. "It wouldn't be the first snake they found."

She nodded and reached for the rail to climb the stairs. "Did they eat bugs when they stayed with you?"

"No, but I did feed them hot dogs. Come on, Jen, you know I wouldn't feed your kids bugs."

"I didn't mean that you fed them bugs. I wondered if you *caught them* eating bugs."

"Never. Why?"

"Oh, something they said." She smiled, letting it go. "Never mind."

"I ate part of a worm once," Adam said as he opened the front door for them. "I turned out okay."

"Thanks, that makes me feel so much better. I want them to grow up to be…" She wouldn't say driven and detached.

"Strong?" He supplied a word that she hadn't planned to say, and she nodded.

"Sure, strong."

The trailer was dark and the furniture was dark. Jenna closed her eyes to give them a second to adjust from bright afternoon sunshine to the shadowy interior of the trailer. When she opened her eyes she could see clearly that it was a mess. Paper plates littered the coffee table and cans of soda sat on the end tables.

"What in the world have you done to this place?" She started gathering trash.

"It's my mess. I can clean it up." He took the paper plates from her hands. "I'm sure not asking you to be my maid."

"You need one."

"Check, please." Clint tapped the paper in his hand and held it out to Adam, who handed the plates back to Jenna.

She grumbled and walked into the kitchen, where the trash was overflowing. Had the man ever picked up after himself? She doubted it. He'd probably always been a superstar, even when he was in diapers.

"Jenna, I'll clean it up later," he called out as he scribbled his signature on a check.

"I don't mind. If we're going to get any work done, I need a clean space to sit down."

"It's clean."

"Give it up, Adam, she's going to win." Words of wisdom from Clint. He smiled at her, winking before he turned his attention back to Adam. "I've lived with her, and she's not going to put up with clutter, trash or dirty dishes. Have you seen her place?"

"I'm right here, stop talking about me." Jenna bumped her fist against her brother's arm. "Don't you have a wife that needs you for something?"

"Yeah, she wants me to do the dishes," Clint admitted with a wry grin.

"I know, when I picked up the boys, she asked me to come down here and make sure you didn't hang out too long." Jenna sat down on the sofa, spreading the catalog she'd brought on the table in front of her. "Time to get busy, Mr. Mackenzie."

"Yeah, busy." He sat down next to her, the sofa cushion sinking a little with his weight. "Where do we start?"

"We'll need to order mattresses, and supplies for the kitchen."

"See you later." Clint paused at the door. "Jen, call me when you get home."

She nodded and waved, not wanting to look at him, to see the worry in his eyes. He was too protective.

And Adam Mackenzie knew it. She felt him slide away, putting space between them. He didn't need to. There was already space between them. His goals. Her need to focus on her boys and living her life.

Those things equaled a chasm the size of the Grand Canyon. And she didn't have any desire or need to close the distance.

Adam's phone buzzed in his shirt pocket. He pulled it out and glanced at a familiar number with a local area code. He slid it back into his pocket and ignored the curious glances of the woman sitting next to him.

"So, we need mattresses. Can we get them in time? What about curtains?" He flipped through the catalog as she wrote down numbers.

"Mini blinds, not curtains. You won't have to take

them down to wash them. I've called a company about mattresses and I think it is doable if we order them today."

"Where am I going to find enough people to work here?"

She put her hand on a page and pointed to a model of mini blind. "That one will work. I measured. It's the right size, a good price and neutral color."

"Okay, back to workers. I need more than help getting the beds made and the lawns mowed."

She pulled a paper out of her pocket. "I know. You need people in the kitchen, a few in the stables, we need cleaning crews before—"

"Could you slow down?" He took off his hat and brushed his hands through his hair. She was smiling at him, that cheeky grin he'd seen a few times. Someone should do something about her cheekiness. Not him.

She was the kind of woman looking for long-term, for a father for her boys. He wasn't the guy she was looking for. He didn't do relationships.

"Of course I can slow down. What's wrong?"

"What do you mean?" He scrambled, wondering if he had missed something. He ran his finger over the catalog, trying to remember what she'd just said.

"You mean, because you're looking dazed, staring at the wall and kind of mumbling?" She laughed a little.

"Have you already planned the entire camp?" He tossed his hat on the nearby chair. She was bossy. He didn't like bossy. It felt like she was taking over his life.

He'd had enough of that. His dad, agents, coaches, a few girlfriends—they'd all had plans for him. Other than Will, he kept a safe distance from people who wanted a piece of the Adam Mackenzie pie.

He knew what she wanted. She wanted this camp. Another of her smiles, this one sheepish. Her eyes were amber and a sprinkling of freckles on her nose caught his attention. She cleared her throat, like she knew the direction his thoughts had taken. "I wrote out a schedule, a tentative menu and how much food I think we'll need and how many workers. I'm not really taking over, just getting you on track."

"Fine, you're hired."

"I didn't ask for a job." She flattened the papers on the table, covering the catalog. "I offered to help. This is volunteering and I'm not asking for anything in return."

Right. He didn't mean to sigh, and he didn't need the look she gave him. But he had a hard time believing she was simply volunteering out of the goodness of her heart.

"You're better suited for this than I am. You take over and I'll go back to Georgia."

"Nope." She stared him down.

He tucked away the strong urge to look deeper into eyes the color of caramel, but flecked with gold. He wouldn't move his hand and slide that strand of hair back behind her ear.

She did it, brushing her hair back and looking away from him.

The camp. He didn't want to run a camp. He wanted to go home before his family caught on, realizing he was a short thirty-minute drive from the home he'd grown up in. He definitely didn't want to take that journey home, not even in his imagination.

A quick look out the window and he saw twin boys following a turtle, their dog barking. That was what a childhood should be.

"Hello, are you still with me? You've forgotten to keep arguing." Her hand was on his arm.

"Sorry, just thinking back. Your boys are having a great childhood. Every kid should have that."

"Which is why you should be excited about this camp. Think of kids coming here, finding turtles, chasing lightning bugs and being kids. Some of them will be able to laugh and play like they've never laughed and played before."

He glanced back out the window, and let her words run through his mind, because she made it feel different. Her words made him think about what this camp meant. It meant children playing, having fun. He could give those kids something every child should have.

It made the pill of running the camp a little less bitter.

His phone buzzed again. He pulled it out and looked at it. Jenna's curious gaze caught his. She didn't ask questions.

"We need to get these orders placed." He picked up her papers she'd taken time to write out. Schedules, workers, menus. He shook his head and folded the papers. "I'll look over these later."

"Okay, but don't put it off. We have a little more than a week."

"Got it."

She held out her hand. "Phone, please. I need to place the order for the mattresses and other things we need in this catalogue."

He handed her his phone. "Do you think I can order the food we'll need from the grocery store?"

"Yeah. But I'd talk to Vera at The Mad Cow. She can look at the menu and the ingredients and make sure you get enough of everything for the amount of kids and workers."

"She won't mind?"

"She won't. I can go with you, if you'd like."

He was starting to feel tied to her. He'd been independent for as long as he could remember and now he needed this woman to keep him on track and help him get things done. That was great for his ego.

Somewhere out there was his life, the one he'd worked hard at building for himself. A house, a life, friends that probably wondered if he'd fallen off the face of the earth and a career he'd been working toward for the last few years.

There were also back issues of magazines and articles categorizing every mistake he'd ever made. Which was why he couldn't leave this mistake undone.

"Adam?"

"I'll stop by tomorrow afternoon and pick you up before I run into town."

"And then we'll go by and speak to Pastor Todd. He has the list of people we can contact for kitchen help, music, activities."

"This is way too much work. I shouldn't let the church bring kids here. We can't have dozens of children roaming this place with nothing to do."

"Have a little faith." She was dialing his phone with the catalog in front of her.

"Yeah, faith."

And then she was talking, ordering dozens of mattresses with his money and giving his credit card number. He felt used all over again, because she wanted this and she was willing to do whatever she needed to do to make it work.

No, she wasn't using him. She was finishing what Billy had started, and what Adam didn't want to finish. He had to remind himself that it had felt good when Billy had asked him for the money to buy this land and start the camp. Billy had sold him on the idea of helping kids.

The camp was a good thing. He stood, leaning against the bar that separated the kitchen from the living area of the trailer and watched Jenna Cameron on his phone, talking, smiling, writing down numbers. Her hair fell forward a little. She had taken it out of the ponytail holder and she pushed it back with a small hand, nails painted light pink.

She'd told him to have faith, and she said it lightly, as if it was a given. Faith was something he hadn't given a lot of thought to over the last ten or fifteen years. Faith was connected to home, to his childhood, and hadn't been included in his adult life.

Why? The question took him by surprise, because he hadn't questioned himself on too many of the choices he'd made. But church. He couldn't remember when he'd stopped going. Maybe college, when he'd realized that he'd had a faith born of his dad's job as pastor. His own connection to God had shorted out.

The trailer was suddenly hot and stuffy. He glanced out the door, to the field, wind blowing the grass that needed to be mowed.

"I'll be outside."

As he walked out the door, he saw the boys playing with the turtle, and the dog sniffing a trail across the open field. The boys turned and ran toward him, not getting that he didn't know a thing about kids.

The phone beeped as Jenna was finishing the order. She switched to the incoming call and then realized she shouldn't have. It wasn't her phone, or her business.

A woman's voice said, "Hello," and then repeated the greeting when Jenna didn't respond. "Adam, don't ignore me. I know you're in Dawson."

"I'm sorry, this isn't Adam." Jenna glanced out the window. "Hold on and I'll get him."

"Who is this?"

"Jenna Cameron. I'm a neighbor."

"No, don't get him."

"It isn't a problem, he's right outside." Jenna stood, revisiting the idea of calling Adam in to get the call. She glanced out the window, watching as he crossed the lawn. "He isn't busy. You can talk to him."

"No, he obviously doesn't want to be bothered by his family, and that's fine." A short pause. "I'm his sister, Elizabeth."

Too much information, too personal. Jenna didn't want to be in the middle of a family problem. She was here because this camp was a good thing. End of story.

"I can give him a message," Jenna offered.

"No, don't give him a message."

"I can give you directions if you want to come by. I'm sure he'd love to see his family."

The sister laughed a little. "You don't know him very well, do you?"

No, she didn't. Jenna glanced out the window again. Adam had David on his shoulders and he was trotting around the yard. She smiled at the sight and wondered about a man who gave piggyback rides to little boys but didn't want to see his own family. Then again, the twins had a way of getting what they wanted. Adam might not be a willing participant in the piggyback rides. As a matter of fact, if she looked closely, he probably looked a little trapped.

"I'll give you directions, in case you change your mind." Jenna continued to watch out the window as she gave the directions and the call ended. And then she regretted what she'd done. A past was a difficult thing to deal with. Jenna knew that as well as anyone.

She also knew that dealing with her childhood had helped her to move forward. She had dealt with her own anger, her resentment of God that had caused her to push away the people who wanted to help.

Maybe, just maybe, that was the reason Adam Mackenzie had crashed into her life.

She walked outside and watched as he switched boys. It was Timmy's turn for a ride on Adam's shoulders. As they went in circles, the dog chased after them, jumping and barking. Jenna leaned on the rail of the porch, watching and worrying. She didn't want for worry to be the emotion she felt.

"The orders are placed," she called out, ending the ride, because she didn't want her boys to be hurt when he left. Adam put Timmy down and walked in her direction, his smile so natural it looked as if it should always be on his face, in his eyes, directed at her. And she knew better than to let her thoughts go there, to think about how good it felt when he smiled at her like that.

For the right woman, that smile would mean everything. It promised things he didn't even realize it promised.

"They're great kids." He had a hand on each of the twins, rubbing their heads and mussing blond hair that needed to be cut.

"They are great. They also need baths. So, you can pick me up tomorrow?"

"I can."

"Guys, time to go." She motioned the boys to her side.

"Do we have to?" Timmy moved with reluctance, shooting a glance back at Adam.

"We have to." Tomorrow she'd leave the boys with Clint and Willow. The less time they spent with Adam the better.

But what about her? How safe was it for her to spend all of this time with a man who planned to leave in six weeks?

Chapter Six

Adam pulled up in front of Jenna's house the next day, parking under the shade of a big oak, and watching as she came out the front door, locking it behind her. She eased herself down the steps and crossed the yard, watching the ground as she walked, but occasionally looking up, smiling at him.

This all felt like a time-out from his life, as if it wasn't even real. It wasn't a vacation, either. But there were good things about all of this. He got out of his truck and walked around to open the door for her, because that's what a gentleman did. His dad had taught him that.

"Where are the boys?" Adam waited for her to get into the truck, but she paused, watching as a car came up her drive. He shifted his gaze in that direction as she answered.

"They're with Clint. He bought a mule and they can't get over the fact that he bought that long-eared thing."

She kept talking. He listened, but the conversation was about the mule being able to jump a fence, the dog chewed up her new rosebush and one of her horses threw a shoe.

"By that, I mean that his shoe came off." She still wasn't getting in the car.

"I know what that means." He stepped to the side as the old sedan pulled up and stopped next to his truck. "Who is that?"

"Jess Lockhart. I'd say we're in trouble. He has his nasty face on."

"Good, we need trouble." Wasn't his life trouble?

Jess Lockhart, a farmer in overalls and work boots, got out of his sedan, still wearing what Jenna had called his nasty face. And he had his angry eyes on to go with it.

"Jess, how are you?" Jenna greeted the man with a smile that was a little tight.

"Well, I'd be a lot better if I knew the rumors I'm hearing around town were wrong."

"What does that mean, Jess?" Jenna tossed her purse into the cab of the truck, like she planned on leaving without finishing the conversation.

"Well, I heard we're going to have a camp with a bunch of juveniles roaming around." Jess turned his censoring gaze on Adam, and Adam was pretty sure he knew what the old farmer meant, and what he was there for.

"I don't think there will be juveniles," Adam defended, and he didn't even care about the camp. He let out a sigh. "The camp isn't a juvenile facility, just a summer camp."

"For kids from the city. They'll be out running through my fields, running my cattle, vandalizing my property."

"Oh, Jess, you know that won't happen." Jenna leaned against the side of the truck, her face a little flushed.

"You can't guarantee it won't, Jenna Cameron. And I plan on stopping it. I'll go to the county commission and I bet they'll find that you don't even have a permit for this thing, or the proper zoning, Adam Mackenzie. I don't care who you think you are, around here that doesn't mean much."

"I'm sure it doesn't." Adam had never felt the truth

to those words quite like he did now. Who he was just didn't really matter. What he wanted mattered even less.

"Jess, take a few days and think about this." Jenna patted the old farmer's arm. "This camp could be such a good thing for kids. It'll keep them off the roads. Remember me when I was sixteen? I bet you wish there'd been a camp to keep me in."

Adam watched the older man change from frowning to smiling, but he didn't think that meant the older man's opinion about the camp had changed. Maybe it didn't matter. Maybe this would put a stop to the camp and Adam would be able to leave without feeling guilty.

"You were a handful, Jenna. You weren't a juvenile delinquent running loose, tearing up my fields."

"Mr. Lockhart, I'm not sure why you think that will happen."

"I watch the news. I know what kids are like today."

"There are good kids, too, Jess." But her soft words weren't working. Adam touched her arm, stopping her.

"I don't want this camp in my backyard." Jess got into his car and slammed the door.

"Well, that went over well, didn't it?" Jenna looked up at him, her smile a little wavering. Adam nodded and he didn't let go of her arm. He knew he couldn't walk away from this camp, not without finishing it. Because it meant a lot to Jenna.

That shouldn't matter to him, it really shouldn't. But it did.

"It went well," he teased, standing behind her as she climbed into the truck. "Don't worry about it. I'll work it out with him."

"Will you? It seems like this would be the perfect opportunity for you to say you tried, but it didn't pan out. You can leave and no one will blame you for going."

"I know." He leaned into the cab of the truck, resting his arms on the roof, and her face was close, close enough that he could smell the light scent of her perfume. "I know I could walk away, but I have a feeling you'd be my biggest nightmare if I did."

He winked and backed away, escaping from whatever had pulled him close to her, whatever it was that made him want to give her this camp, and make her smile.

"Let's go to lunch." He hadn't planned on offering the invitation, but it was close to noon.

"I don't know."

"We can sit at separate tables if you're worried about what people will say."

She smiled, a little sheepish and kind of shy. He shifted and pulled onto the road. Two miles to Dawson. Two miles of her sitting next to him, his mind framing a picture of a woman with a smile that he wouldn't soon forget.

"I guess you can sit with me." She looked out the window. "But you can't talk to me."

"Okay, that's a deal."

"You know I'm kidding, right? And besides that, we need to start at The Mad Cow, so Vera can help us with the specifics of the menu before we go to the store. We have to get this done before kids show up."

"I do know you're kidding, and yes, we have to get this done." He shifted again, slowing as they turned from the paved road they lived on, onto the highway that led to Dawson.

"We could have brought the boys." He wondered why she had decided to leave them with her brother.

"We can do this without them. It'll be easier."

"Okay." He accelerated and the tires hummed on the road. The wind whipped through the cab of the truck and Jenna rolled the window up.

"Adam, they're little boys and you're a hero who isn't going to be here long. I don't want…"

She looked away, brushing a hand through long hair that had gotten tangled by the wind.

"You don't want them to be upset when I leave?" He got it. He should have thought of it himself. They weren't a couple, the boys knew that, but boys got attached to people. They could even get attached to him.

He could get attached to them. That thought took him by surprise. He shifted gears and let the feelings go, because this wasn't real. This was Oklahoma in the summer, a return to his youth for a few short weeks, and soon he'd return to reality.

The woman next to him was a reminder that this was reality. She sang along to the radio and her scent, peaches and soap, filled the cab of the truck, whipping around him with the breeze from his open window.

He slowed the truck as they drove into Dawson, a true one-horse town. That horse was in the pen behind the first house inside the city limits, munching on a round bale of hay. The main street had only a few businesses. A convenience store, a farm store where they sold a few groceries, farm supplies and grain, and at the corner of Main and Dairy Road was The Mad Cow Café. The name of the restaurant had been painted on the side of the building in big, black-and-white-spotted block letters.

Getting attached. He glanced in Jenna's direction as he pulled into the parking lot of The Mad Cow. He could get attached to her.

She didn't beat around the bush, saying only what he wanted to hear. She was honest, blunt and sometimes shy. When she wanted something from him, this camp, she spelled it out and told him why.

He set the emergency brake and pulled the keys out of the ignition. Jenna was already opening her door, like nothing had happened, like getting attached wasn't an issue for her.

Maybe it wasn't.

Jenna noticed the crowd inside The Mad Cow, but she didn't mention it. Really, why should it matter? So what if people glanced out the window at them, or mouths moved as questions were asked behind hands.

He had more to worry about than she did. People knew him, knew his family, and knew what he'd accomplished since he'd left Oklahoma.

For years she'd kept this town fed with gossip, someone to talk about. Her antics had been reported in church prayer groups, at the quilting bee and right here at The Mad Cow on Monday mornings.

It didn't bother her at all that he was the "something to talk about" now. He had broad shoulders. He could handle it.

Broad shoulders and a hand that casually brushed hers as they walked across the parking lot. What would that feel like, to hold his hand? She shoved her hands into her pockets.

He pushed the door of the diner open and she walked in ahead of him. A few people turned to stare, to smile, to greet them.

"Jenna, how're the kids?" Opal, the hostess and waitress, hurried past with a coffeepot and a pen shoved through her thick, gray hair.

One of the regulars yelled at her to take his order.

"I'll give you an order," Opal bit back. "How about a full order of hush-it-up, with a side of bite-your-tongue?"

Opal turned her attention back to Jenna and Adam.

"I tell you, this crowd gets more attitude in the summer. Must be the heat. Anyway, about the boys…"

"They're great. Clint has them for the day."

"Good, sweetie. He's a doll for giving you a break. You have a seat over there by the window. Take the booth that isn't in the sun or you'll be hotter than a flitter."

"Flitter?" Adam whispered in her ear.

She brushed him off and she didn't let herself smile.

"How're your horses, Jenna?" Gary Walker set his coffee cup down on the table. "Do you still have that gray?"

Jenna stopped at the table to talk to the farmer. "I still have him. Are you still interested?"

"I might be, let me do some figurin' on it."

A hand touched her arm. Adam's hand as he slid past her. He leaned, his mouth close to her ear. "What's a *flitter?*"

Laughter bounced around inside and she looked away, trying to ignore the look on his face, the ornery arch of his brows, the quirk of his mouth.

"Well?" He slid into the booth, sitting across the table from her. "Oh, it is okay if we sit together, right?"

"It's okay, and stop asking me what it is."

"You don't know?"

"Of course I don't. No one really knows what it is. It's just hotter than one, and sometimes someone is as ornery as one. Like you. You're as ornery as a flitter." She leaned toward him. "I think it might be a kind of pancake or something, but I've always been too embarrassed to ask. Do you want to ask someone?"

He leaned back in his seat and laughed. "No, I don't want to ask."

Opal was back with two ice waters and the coffeepot. "What can I get the two of you?" She poured coffee.

"Pancakes for me." Jenna handed the menu back without looking at it.

"Pancakes for lunch?" Adam, still looking at his menu, glanced up.

"They serve breakfast all day."

"I think I'll have pancakes, too." He smiled up at Opal. "Make mine a double."

He was stirring sugar into his coffee when Vera walked through the door of the kitchen and saw them. Her eyes lit up, and he thought it had more to do with the fact that Jenna was with him than with her delight at having him in her restaurant.

Jenna had lived through more than he could imagine. And he'd used his childhood as a crutch for years. He could admit that. His dad had pushed him hard. Adam had been pushed in school, pushed in church and pushed into football. Or maybe he had started out as a kid wanting to play.

Too many years had passed to remember.

"How are you kids?" Vera sat down next to Jenna, her hair in a net and perspiration beaded along her brow. "My goodness, it has been busy today. But that isn't why you're here. Do you have a list for food, Jenna?"

She dug around in her purse and pulled out a piece of paper. "I have a menu that I think might work. I'm not sure how much we'll need for fifty kids and staff."

"I'll give this a look-see and let you know what I think." She nodded as she read what Jenna had written down. A menu he hadn't even seen. "I know from experience working for the school that we need the right combination of foods. That food pyramid, you know. We want to make sure we're close to meeting it with the menu."

"I hadn't thought of that." Jenna turned a little pink. "I was just trying to think of stuff they'd like."

"This all looks good. Have the two of you ordered?"

"We have." Adam watched the two women, wondering what else they could cook up, and trying to calculate how much this would cost him. He'd transferred money to the camp account this morning, preparing himself for the inevitable.

"You do know that Jess is stirring up trouble, right?" Vera looked at Jenna, but the words were for Adam, and he knew it.

"He stopped by my house," Jenna answered for him.

"I was afraid he might. He's a mess, that man. He's just bored and lonely since Lucy passed."

"But he can't stop the camp, Vera." Jenna shook her head. "I'll talk him out of it."

Adam let them talk, let them plan, but a part of him thought about the relief it would be if Jess Lockhart managed to stop the camp from becoming a reality. He could sell the land and go back to Atlanta, without guilt, without anyone to blame him. He would have tried.

Unfortunately they were talking about ordering food, and that meant, for the time being, he wasn't going anywhere.

Adam was on the phone with Will when cars started rolling up the drive two days after he and Jenna had ordered food from the grocery store. He watched from the kitchen window, amazed by the people, and by the woman who had pulled this off. Her truck was the first in the line of vehicles pulling to a stop out front.

"What's up?" Will's voice reminded him that he was on the phone.

"The help we arranged on our trip to town has arrived. It's like someone called in the cavalry."

"Imagine that." Humor laced Will's tone, and a little of that I-told-you-so attitude was evident. "Adam, this is going to be a good thing, a gold star on your résumé."

Adam walked out the front door. It was already hot and the humidity in the air felt like it might be hitting a hundred and five percent.

"I'm a little old for gold stars, don't you think?"

"You have enough demerits. A gold star won't hurt when we go in for that job interview."

Demerits. Things he'd done that he regretted. Scuffles, too many late nights, too much hard living. For the last few years he'd stayed away from those places, things that could get him into trouble. People didn't remember the good Adam; they kept going back to the wild, twentysomething Adam.

"You got the appointment set up?" He brought it back to the job, not the past.

"It's set up. But let me tell you, it wasn't easy. These guys appreciate that your name will draw viewers to any program you're broadcasting, but they don't want bad publicity on their watch."

"Is that a warning?" He leaned against the rail of the porch and watched as Jenna got out of her truck. The boys weren't with her again. He felt a strange twist that could have been disappointment.

He hadn't expected to miss those two kids. He told himself he should be glad they weren't there, getting into trouble, finding snakes. Or eating bugs. He smiled.

"Not a warning," Will said, "just a word of caution to keep out of trouble."

"You know I'll stay out of trouble. What trouble can a guy get into in Dawson, Oklahoma?"

"I'm sure there's trouble to be found."

Trouble. Adam's gaze lingered on Jenna Cameron as

she got out of her truck. He'd met trouble before and she looked like the real deal. She looked like a cowgirl that could get under a man's skin and make him think about promises, and forever. If a man was so inclined. He wasn't.

He had dated a lot. He hadn't treated the women badly. He hadn't hurt anyone. He'd just kept it simple and protected himself from entanglements and women who wanted to use him.

Or at least that's the life he'd lived for the last few years. Since Paula. He'd never admit she broke his heart. He could admit she'd temporarily broken his bank account. For a few months he'd really thought he'd found the woman who loved him, not his career, not the spotlight.

He'd been wrong.

Jenna walked up to the sedan that parked next to her truck. Adam slipped his phone back into his pocket, wondering if he'd ended his call with Will. Jenna nodded in his direction and smiled a faint smile. As he crossed the lawn, she headed toward him, halting once.

"Help has arrived." She waved her arm to include the cars and trucks that had lined up in the drive, some pulling off into the grass to park.

"Yes, this definitely looks like help." He turned at the sound of a tractor heading in their direction.

"That would be Clint with his Brush Hog. It'll get this place mowed in no time."

A tractor with a mower that would cut swaths a good five feet wide. He liked that idea. But the wheels in his mind were turning as he watched people get out of their cars.

"What was that look for?" Jenna's hand slipped through his arm and he didn't object. He looked away, pretending not to notice that she leaned against him, her grip on his arm tightening.

"What look?" he said, pasting a smile in place of the frown she must have noticed.

"The I'm-about-to-get-taken-to-the-cleaners look."

Had she really seen that in his expression? Had he gotten that cynical? He looked down, and he smiled because she was smiling at him. But he *had* gotten that cynical. He did expect to be used. The reality of that thought knotted in his stomach.

He didn't like seeing himself in a way he hadn't seen himself before. He didn't like looking at himself through Jenna Cameron's eyes.

"I had a budget for this place and the budget is pretty much used up, thanks to Billy," he admitted.

"Adam, this is a community and what you're doing will help kids here as well as outside the community. We're all here to be a part of that, no strings. Not for you, but for those kids."

"Ouch."

"Ah, did that bruise your ego?"

"Only a little."

"Do you really need for this to be all about you?"

"You are about the most scrappy female I've ever met. No, I don't need for this to be about me. I'm just…"

"It's okay. Now you know that we're just here to help, so let's get busy. Pastor Todd is going to be a big help. He was a youth minister for years and organized retreats and camps."

She nodded toward the pastor who had gotten out of his car. Jenna's hand slipped off his arm and she took a few steps, then waited for him to join her. Time to get started. Time to be involved in this camp and this community.

Six months ago, when he'd undertaken this venture, it had been Billy's camp and Adam's money. It had been about a tax write-off and something good on his résumé. He wouldn't have to show up, except once in a while for a photo opportunity.

And here he was, in charge.

No, not really in charge. He was the owner, but Jenna Cameron was definitely in charge.

Jenna couldn't stop smiling as she watched people getting out of their cars. The men had tool boxes, the women had cleaning supplies. She was so proud of her church, her community. She could think that now, with troubled years behind her and turbulent waters long under the bridge.

Ten-year-old Jenna had avoided these people like the plague. They were the people who had stopped by with casseroles when her mom died, or had pulled up in the drive and honked on Sunday mornings, wanting her to attend church and then driving away with Clint when she would no longer go, not in torn jeans and holey sneakers, tangled rats in her hair.

She had listened to her father talk about self-righteous people wanting to look down their noses at the Cameron family and turn them into a charity case. She had groomed resentment like a well-tended garden and fought hard against everyone, including God. She had fought against the cookies, hugs and stories of Jesus.

All the while, these people really were waiting to love her. And now they were here to help Adam, and to help kids they didn't even know.

"You okay?" Adam asked. The velvet and thunder tones in his voice sent a chill down her spine.

"I'm fine, why?"

"You stopped walking. You seem a little down today."

She looked up, meeting a deep look on his face that didn't tease. That look said he understood because maybe he'd felt this way himself. Of course he had; it was the look she'd noticed in his eyes when a game ended and reporters circled him, wanting to know how it felt to be him.

She had always thought that maybe it didn't feel as good as the world imagined. He was still waiting for an answer to his question.

"I'm fine, a little sore today." She rarely admitted that, because the words, once spoken, made it real.

Flashbacks happened, sometimes even in the bright sunlight of a summer day in Oklahoma. Sometimes she could smell the smoke, the blood, the dark mustiness of that closet where she'd been hidden.

Sometimes in the dark of night she wanted to scream for daylight.

Sometimes she wanted her life back, the hope and promise of marriage and love, a family. And then she fought it all back and she remembered faith and meeting God in that dark room, knowing He wouldn't let her down, believing He would get her home. Home to her family, to her boys.

He had. And she hadn't been let down. She could get through anything.

"You're fine." Adam's tone said he didn't believe her. "Pastor Todd, good to see you again."

He was good at pushing past pain, too. She knew a kindred spirit when she met one. He was smiling again, letting go of their conversation.

"Good to see you, too. I've got delivery dates for the food. The kitchen help is going to get the pans and dishes organized and we'll make out a work schedule." Pastor Todd fell in next to Adam and they, along with the group of church members, moved toward the kitchen.

Vera joined them, in jeans and a T-shirt today, not her

customary smock apron. "I've got a schedule for the kitchen. I won't be able to be here to help, but I've got a sister, Louisa, who has helped me a lot in the restaurant. She's going to be in charge of cooking. Charm Jones is going to be in charge of servers and dishes. They'll make sure you have plenty of people on hand."

"Okay." Adam's tight smile didn't faze Vera. She had a list and she was ticking things off.

"And Gordon Flynn is bringing beef over from the packing plant. He's giving you a good deal on half a beef."

"Half a beef?" Adam's smile disappeared.

"Oh, honey, that's not all," Vera continued, as if she didn't notice his surprise. Or was it outrage? "We're also having chicken one night, and then there'll be sausage and eggs for breakfast."

A heavy sigh from Adam. Jenna felt a little bad for him. He was probably envisioning his savings account dwindling, or maybe felt as if the community had hijacked him and his camp.

"Adam, a lot of the cost is being covered by the church."

That got his attention. He glanced from her to Pastor Todd.

"We want to help." Pastor Todd nodded in the direction of the chapel. "This camp is something the area needs. And the community should be a part of it. Our churches need to be a part of reaching out to the children who come here."

"That doesn't mean you get out of the work. We'll need your help hanging the mini blinds." Jenna nudged Adam with her elbow, hoping to ease the tightened lines around his mouth. "You probably won't even need a ladder."

Chapter Seven

Adam stood on the ladder, on the second floor of the dorm, attaching the first mini blind on the window. The older woman standing on the floor next to the ladder held the tools and the hardware for the blinds. She made a noise and he thought she might have said something.

"I'm sorry?" He looked down and the ladder shook a little. He held his breath and waited for it to stop weaving. Or maybe he was weaving, not the ladder. He started to close his eyes but knew from experience that would only make it worse.

Worse, being on the second floor, looking out the window at the ground. It seemed to be fifty feet down, and he knew it wasn't. He focused on the floor. On the woman helping him. She shrugged and her brows arched and drew in.

He was sure she'd said something.

"What?" She didn't smile.

He started to work again and again heard her mutter. "Did you say something?"

"No, of course not."

"Am I doing something wrong?"

She bit down on her lip and shook her head and that didn't convince him. "No, you're fine."

That tone. Of course he was doing something wrong. He wasn't a handyman. He didn't fix things. He played football. His home-repair skills were pretty limited.

"Mrs. Glenn, if I'm doing something wrong, please tell me." He counted to ten because he was about to lose his loose grip on what patience he had left. The lady watching him, gray hair permed into tight curls and T-shirt stating that everything she did was done for Jesus, was the woman pushing him to the end of his rope. And occasionally bumping the ladder he didn't really want to be standing on.

"Okay, I don't mean to be bossy, because this is your camp and your dorm, but it would be better if you put those blinds on the inside of the window frame, not on the outside. It'll just look a lot nicer."

"It isn't easier, though."

"Well, no, of course not." She frowned and shook her head. "Life isn't always about taking the easy way."

One, two, three, four, five… Counting wasn't helping. Adam closed his eyes and felt like he was swaying, about to fall. He grabbed the ladder and sucked in a deep breath.

"Are you afraid of heights?" The pleasant voice of Mrs. Glenn, sounding a little amused and tinkly. He got the impression that his fear made her day.

"No, of course not." He looked down and her eyes had widened and her smile beamed.

"I think you are." She pointed to the ground, and he knew she'd been waiting for an opportunity like this one. "Let me do that and you hold the tools."

"I really can do this." He unscrewed the bracket that he'd put on the outside of the window frame. He was a man. He could conquer a ladder. He could hang a mini blind.

He could grunt like Tim Allen, if need be.

"Of course you can." She backed away from the ladder.

Adam gave up. He climbed down the wobbly ladder and, when his feet touched the ground, he sighed, and he hadn't meant to sigh. Man, he hated ladders. And Mrs. Glenn loved that fact. She smiled as she handed him the tools she'd been holding.

"We'll have this done in no time. Now, you get the blinds out of that box while I get these brackets attached."

Screws went between her teeth, the tools slid into her pockets and she was up the ladder, happy as a lark. No more muttering. No more disapproving looks. If he'd known it was that easy to get her approval, he never would have gone up that ladder.

To prove he wasn't totally inept, he started taking blinds out of boxes and handing her what she asked for. They were on the fourth window when footsteps behind him caught his attention.

"Lunchtime." Jenna's soft drawl.

"Already?" He glanced over his shoulder, at the woman standing behind him, hair in a ponytail and clear gloss on her lips.

"Yep. Food is in the kitchen. Looks like you're getting the blinds up with no problem." Jenna smiled at Mrs. Glenn, who stood on the ladder, precarious and not caring.

"We have a system that works well." Mrs. Glenn pulled a screw out of her mouth and pushed it into the bracket.

Adam waited for her to mention the fact that she had discovered his fear. Instead she finished the window and climbed down. She set the tools back in the box and dusted her hands off on her jeans.

"You're doing great." Jenna shot him a look that he ignored.

"We should probably head for the kitchen." Mrs. Glenn was ahead of them, nearly to the door. "I have sugar issues. I need to eat every three hours."

"Of course, I'd forgotten." Jenna smiled. "We're heading that way, too."

But slower than Mrs. Glenn, Adam realized. Mrs. Glenn obviously needed to eat soon. He watched as she hightailed it across the newly mowed lawn, in the direction of the metal building that housed the kitchen.

He liked the layout of the camp. There was a central yard. On the west side of the lawn was the barn and corral, east was the kitchen, south was the dorm. Behind the dorm an open-air chapel had been built.

Horses grazed in the fields, tails swishing to brush away the flies. He'd forgotten what it was like here, in Oklahoma. He'd forgotten the rolling fields, the smell of freshly mowed hay. He'd forgotten the way the setting sun touched the horizon and turned everything gold in the evenings.

It didn't matter, though, because he wasn't staying.

"The beds are being put together and the bathrooms are clean." Jenna offered the progress report as they crossed the lawn. He'd forgotten the sweetness of a country girl on a summer afternoon. "Willow brought the boys by. She has to take the baby to the pediatrician."

"Is the baby sick?"

"Not really, just a cough. But Willow's a first-time parent and she's a little worried. She lost her hearing from meningitis."

"That happens?"

"Not often, but it can." She limped next to him, and

he wasn't thinking about Willow, but about the woman at his side. And he knew she wouldn't want to discuss what was happening with her. He knew, because he thought they might be a lot alike.

He touched her hand, by accident, and her fingers brushed his, but then moved away, almost as if she had considered holding his hand and wouldn't. And she shouldn't, not if she wanted to protect her heart. He knew that as well as anyone.

The aroma wafting from the open windows of the kitchen were a welcome distraction. He opened the door and motioned Jenna inside.

"Where are the boys?" He glanced around the open room with the long tables and the open kitchen area with a counter full of warmers and steaming food. He had expected sandwiches today, not a buffet.

"They ate with Willow. She took them to town for pizza. But they also had half a peanut butter sandwich a little while ago. Now they're outside, playing."

"Oh, so are they okay outside?"

She pointed out the window. The boys were playing in the yard with trucks, obviously okay. "We can see them from here. If they leave that spot, we'll worry."

At that age, he wouldn't have stayed in one spot. He kind of figured the twins wouldn't be there for long. It wasn't his business, though. He grabbed a tray and followed the woman whose business it was.

"Stop looking out the window." She had her back to him, so how did she know? She turned and smiled. "I can almost feel you tensing up back there, wondering what they'll get into. They're almost six, they're old enough to play in the yard, especially since we're right here, watching them."

"I know that."

"You're going to be a nervous wreck by the time this camp is over."

"Which is why I should just sign it over to the church and be done with it." He plopped potatoes on his plate and drenched them with gravy.

"That would be the easy way out, wouldn't it?"

Of course it would. Watching her, he wondered if she had ever opted for the easy way.

"Yes, it would be," he admitted, and followed her to a table that was already crowded. He wanted a corner booth and no one staring. He wasn't going to get that either. From across the table she smiled at him.

He glanced out the window, at the boys.

Jenna tapped his hand. "They're still there."

"Yes, they are." He cut his meat loaf and dipped it in gravy. "This is good."

"Vera's secret recipe. Don't ask what she puts in it. She doesn't mind sharing the packets of seasoning she makes up, but she won't tell you what's in it."

"No MSG, right?"

She looked up and shook her head. "You're a mess. Just eat."

He ate a few more bites, and then glanced out the window again. Jenna followed his look and her eyes widened.

"They're gone," he announced, standing as she stood. "I'll go check on them."

"I can do it." She headed for the door and he followed.

The boys were nowhere to be seen. They couldn't have disappeared that fast. Adam left Jenna standing in the yard and hurried toward the stable and the horses. That's when he saw them.

"They're on the pony." Jenna had seen them at the same time and her anxious shout didn't help to calm his nerves. She was the one who didn't let things bother her.

But bothered was a good way to feel when he knew the boys were in serious trouble. They were on a spotted pony, bareback and with nothing but a rope around the animal's neck. How in the world had they managed to get in this much trouble, this quick?

And they didn't even seem to know the trouble they were in. They had sticks and were obviously fast on the trail of bad guys, the little horse obliging them by picking up his legs in a fast trot. The boys were bouncing and holding tight with sun-browned legs wrapped around the pony's round little belly.

"Timmy! David!" Jenna had caught up with him, her chest heaving a little with the exertion. "Stop that pony now!"

The boys waved.

"They're going to get thrown." Adam couldn't help but growl the words.

"They're not." But she didn't sound as positive as he would have liked. "Let's walk slowly and not scare the pony. The boys know how to ride, they'll be okay."

Walk slowly, don't run and grab the boys off the pony. He wanted to take her advice, but he couldn't. "I'm sorry, I've got to get them off her."

The boys were ripping across the lawn on the horse. Jenna grabbed his arm. "Okay, go get them, but be careful not to spook the pony."

The boys were bouncing along on the back of the pony. The door to the kitchen had opened and Adam knew they had an audience. Pastor Todd and the church members who were still there had joined Jenna.

Adam walked fast, toward the pony and the boys. The little pony stopped and ducked her head to pull at a bite of red clover. As soon as she had it in her mouth, she took off again. Adam was starting to think she was in on the orneriness. She wasn't a victim of those boys, she was the coconspirator.

"Lady Bug, here, come here." He didn't shout, but the name got the attention of the spotted pony. She flicked her ears and looked at him, but then her ears went back. "Guys, pull back on your rope and stop her."

The twins nodded, but they didn't look convinced. They smiled at him as if they were having the time of their lives. And he had to wonder if he wouldn't have felt the same way. A smile and then a chuckle sneaked up on him. It was harder to be stern the next time he called out to them.

"Come on, when she stops again, you guys climb off. You're scaring your mom." And ten years off his life.

David glanced over his shoulder and made eye contact with Adam. The kid looked a little worried. Either he didn't want to get in trouble, or he was afraid of getting thrown. His blond hair was tousled and his little face was smudged with dirt and peanut butter. Adam was nearly close enough to grab the pony.

And then she lunged, Timmy encouraging her with a foot tap to her side. Adam ran, because this was no longer a game. He caught up with the little mare just short of a stand of cedars with low limbs that would brush the boys off if the pony decided to keep going. Rather than grabbing her, he grabbed the twins off her back.

They hugged his neck and he took a deep breath. Man, he was out of shape, or maybe it was fear. His lungs heaved for oxygen and his heart raced. He hugged the boys, one on each hip, and turned back in the direction they'd come. He could see Jenna standing with Pastor Todd, saw her hands come together and then cover her face.

One of the other men headed in the direction of the pony, a bucket of grain in his hand.

"You boys shouldn't do that to your mom. From now on, if you want to ride, you ask. You don't get on a horse without permission. You could get hurt doing that."

"I told you so," David muttered and glared, gray eyes narrowed at Timmy.

"You're always a chicken."

"Buddy, doing the right thing doesn't make a guy a chicken." Adam put the boys down and took them by the hand to finish the walk. Timmy tried to get loose. Adam kept hold of his little hand.

And Jenna was walking toward them, looking like he might be her favorite person in the world—for the moment. She didn't know him that well, and he planned on keeping it that way. Let her think he was a hero, not a jaded athlete who wouldn't stay long enough for her to really get to know him.

"I'm taking the two of you home. Adam, I hate to leave, but you have plenty of help and these guys are going to be spending time in their room, not playing."

"I understand. Do you need help getting them in the truck?"

She shook her head. "I can manage. Besides, I think that's Jess driving down the road. Probably with more complaints about the camp."

He thought she was probably right, but as she walked away, Jess wasn't on his mind. She was.

"Bologna sandwiches for supper tonight, guys." Jenna walked through the back door and the boys looked up. They were sitting at the kitchen table, looking at books, because she wouldn't let them play.

For the last two hours, since she'd left the camp with them, they'd been confined to the house and only allowed to do what she approved. While she'd gone out to feed her horses, the selected activity had been looking at books.

Her poor horses. Monday she really had to stay at home and do some work with them. She had a gelding that she needed to sell at the end of the month. He was nearly ready to be used in reigning competitions.

"Bologna sandwiches?" Timmy wrinkled his nose at her dinner suggestion and brought her mind back to the kitchen and her dinner preparations. "Can I have cheese and crackers?"

"You can. And grapes." At least if they ate grapes she'd feel like they were eating something healthy.

David wrinkled his nose when she said grapes. She sighed.

"What is it, buddy?"

"Do I have to eat grapes?"

"Carrots?" she offered as she poured herself a glass of tea. "Or an apple."

He bit down on his bottom lip and stared at the floor. When he looked up, his eyes were watery. "There aren't any apples."

"I had a whole bag." She really needed to sit down. Pain was shooting up her leg, biting sharp, and her back ached.

"I kinda fed them to Charlie."

Jenna sat down. "Kinda? You fed them to your horse? All of them?"

He nodded. "He liked 'em a lot."

"Oh, David, honey, we need to check and make sure you didn't make him sick. You guys go clean up before we eat and I'll check on Charlie."

"Sorry, Mom." David kissed her cheek. "I can check on him."

She hugged him and she didn't sigh. "It's okay. I'll check on him."

He sounded so big, and she knew someday he would be a good man. She was raising good men. It meant everything to her. Protecting them meant everything. They had been left by too many people. They had almost lost her.

She tried to block the image of that moment earlier in the day when Adam had held both of her boys, and they had clung to him. He would leave them. After the camp was off the ground and running, he would go back to his life. The life that was so far removed from theirs, she couldn't imagine all of the differences. Once he returned, he would never think of them again.

Not that he needed to think of her. He was a blip on the radar screen of her life. She had two main priorities: Timmy and David. She had watched them cry when their dad left after his last visit, telling her he would send child support, but his life wasn't about her or the boys.

They hadn't seen him for three years. He was remarried, living in California. Someday she knew they'd want to know him. Maybe someday he'd want to see them again.

Six months ago she had seen the confusion on their faces when they asked about Jeff, the man she'd planned to marry. She'd had to explain that he wasn't going to be seeing them anymore.

Her life, her recovery, was too much reality for a guy that wanted to stay young a little while longer. Sometimes she wished she could have stayed young longer. There were days that she felt twenty years older than her twenty-seven years. She felt like she'd lived a lifetime in the last seven of those years.

She remembered what it was like to feel pretty. She hadn't felt pretty in a long, long time. She couldn't remember getting dressed up for a date, or the way it felt to put on something other than flat-heeled cowboy boots or tennis shoes.

But she didn't have time to feel sorry for herself.

"Be right back, guys." She stopped at the door and looked back at them. They were on a stool at the sink, washing their hands. "Don't get into anything."

Wishful thinking on her part.

Chapter Eight

"Jenna, are you out here?" Adam walked into the barn, peering into the dark shadows. He'd been in the house for five minutes, waiting for her to come in, to feed the boys.

"Jen?"

"Jenna. No one calls me Jen but Clint." She was sitting outside a stall, looking inside the darkened cubicle. He peeked around the corner of the gate and saw the pony, bloated belly and head hanging.

"What's up?" He leaned against the post, looking at her, and then at the pony. They both—her and the pony—looked pretty miserable. He knew enough about women to know that the word *miserable* wasn't one that she wanted attached to her appearance.

"David fed his pony a bag of apples. I think Charlie is going to be okay, but I wanted to make sure. He's pretty uncomfortable, the little pig."

"How about you? You okay?"

She looked up, eyes dark, shadowy. Her nose was pink and her face was a little puffy. He wouldn't ask. He didn't want to go there. He had a rule about women, nothing personal. Go out to dinner, take a walk in the park, go to a show, but never ask personal questions.

Too late, he realized that his question was personal. He hadn't asked about her tears, but he'd gone far enough. Her eyes watered a little and she shrugged. But then she didn't answer.

"I'm fine, just a little tired."

"That's my fault." He reached for a bucket and turned it over to use it as a seat.

"Not really. I've just been pushing myself a little too much lately."

"The boys told me they're having bologna sandwiches for supper."

"Tattletales." She smiled.

"Yeah, I called from town." He took off his hat and ran a hand through his hair. It was getting shaggy. "I brought food from The Mad Cow."

"You didn't have to do that. Bologna sandwiches won't hurt them."

"Too late, it's done. So why don't we go inside and eat before the food gets cold. I can come back out before I leave."

"Okay." She stood, wobbling a little. She reached for the gate and held it a minute before pushing it closed.

Her first step was tentative, and he didn't know what to do, or how to offer help.

"You going to make it to the house?"

"Of course I am." She took another step, this one looking more painful than the last. A single tear trickled down her cheek but she looked up at him, smiling. "It might take a while."

"I'll be back in a minute."

"Where are you…"

"Right back."

He jogged to the house and found what he was looking for in a corner of the laundry room. When he returned, she was sitting on the stool. Charlie was still moping in a corner of the stall.

Adam opened the wheelchair and pointed. She glanced up, her cheeks pink.

"I assume this is yours?" He waited, holding the handles. "Come on, I'm a football player, I know how to drive one of these."

"I know." She sniffed a little as she stood up. "I want this in my past, not here, today."

"I could carry you." He winked, and she smiled a little, another tear trickling down her cheek. Tears were not his thing, especially soft tears that someone fought, trying to be strong. Hers weren't the wailing, I-want-my-way kind of tears. Hers were about being strong, but feeling weak.

And he didn't have a handkerchief.

"No, I think I can do without you carrying me." She moved to the seat and hunched forward a little. And he didn't want her to feel weak. "This isn't the past, is it? It's my life. One moment and everything changed forever."

He pushed her out of the barn. The sun was setting and the sky was pink. The trees were dark green silhouettes against the twilight sky. He maneuvered over rough ground, big rocks and clumps of grass.

"Moments do that to us." He pushed the chair over a rut. "Moments can change everything. That's life. A moment and my cousin was gone and I'm here. I know that isn't a moment on a dusty road in Iraq, but it's the moment that brought me home."

"With me," she whispered. "I'm sorry, that isn't what I meant. I'm just saying, this probably isn't where you expected to be, either. If you weren't here, where would you be tonight?"

"Saturday night in Atlanta?" He laughed because he didn't want to answer. "Probably not somewhere I'd be proud of."

"Life has taken you a long way from Oklahoma, hasn't it?"

"Life does that. This wasn't what I wanted—this land, the farms, the country. I worked my entire life to be where I am, doing what I've done, going where I'm going in my career."

"I'm not sure what I wanted before."

"What do you want now?"

She looked back, her hair brushing the back of the seat. "I want to raise my boys. I want to be a good mom. I want to survive this and be strong. That's about it."

"I think you're achieving your goals. You have great kids. You are strong." He was staring at the back of her head and he could see her hands clasped together in her lap.

The back door opened and Timmy pushed it wide, stepping out to hold it for them to enter. The kid didn't even look worried. Her boys had accepted their lives, too.

Adam respected that. He'd never been good at accepting. Sometimes it felt like he'd been fighting his entire life.

Today wasn't any different. Today he was fighting the urge to kiss a woman from Oklahoma. He was fighting the urge to promise her things would get better. Those weren't his promises to make. The best he could do was provide a meal.

He parked her at the table and left her to get the tea he'd already poured for them. The boys raced out of the room, obviously relieved from their punishment.

Adam watched them go, shaking his head because

they were all about life, playing and loving their mom. That probably wasn't hard for them to do, the loving Jenna part.

Jenna looked at her kitchen. The boys had already eaten. The takeout containers were open on the table, and mostly empty. The dog had run into the kitchen and was trying to nose his way onto the table, like he thought no one would notice.

"Dog, get." Jenna shooed him away, wheeling closer to the table and smelling fried chicken from The Mad Cow.

"Do you want tea?"

She turned. Adam had two glasses. One for him, one for her. Or that was her guess. He was staying? She felt weak inside, and he was staying.

"You know, I can take it from here. If you have somewhere you need to go."

"Are you trying to get rid of me?" He set two glasses on the table and opened a container.

"No, I just know that you have a lot to get done in the next few days."

"The help I got today made a big dent in that."

"It's all coming together." She dug her fork into the chicken and took a bite. Adam was watching, his own meal in front of him.

"Yeah, it is." He leaned back in his chair, watching her, and she wasn't hungry. "But then what? Let it run its course for the summer, and then put it up for sale?"

"Or you could keep it going. You could be really good for the camp and the kids. Even if you ran it from Atlanta."

"I don't think so. I'm not a role model or a camp director."

"You're not so bad."

His brows went up. "Yes, I am."

She smiled, shaking her head in disagreement with him, because she thought he had a kind heart that he'd been keeping tucked away, protected.

"Oh, what did Jess want?"

"Same as before. He wanted to give me a second chance to back out on this camp. Pastor Todd tried to talk to him, but he wouldn't listen. He said Pastor Todd has a history of bringing in strays, so why would Jess trust his judgment."

"I wouldn't worry. Jess will give it up."

"He's going to talk to the county planning and zoning committee."

"We'll have to pray."

"Right."

Jenna pushed her plate away, because she wasn't really hungry. "What happened to you?"

He looked up, no smile, just a look in his eyes that was soft, a little wounded. "What does that mean?"

"You know what I mean. What turned you against God?"

"I don't have anything against God. I attended church my entire childhood."

"And now?"

"I don't think anything happened. I left home." He shrugged and looked away. "I think I enjoyed the freedom of college a little too much. I was busy with football, busy with my social life."

"And no one to tell you to slow down."

"For the first time in my life. That kind of freedom can be a dangerous thing." He grinned a little. "I can't say that I'm proud of that, or how far I've gone from my roots."

"I guess I don't know your roots."

"Pastor's kid. And a dad who almost made the pros, but didn't."

She had missed that part of his bio.

But now she got it. She knew the secret to who he was, the look she'd seen in his eyes. "You thought you weren't good enough."

"I didn't say that."

"No, you didn't, but I'm right. You were a hero, from a good family, and you didn't feel any better about yourself than I did as a kid."

"Maybe. Why does it matter so much to you?"

Heat crawled up her neck and she looked down, at the napkin scrunched up in her hand. "I've watched you and I've wondered what your story was."

"Now you know." He stood, and after standing next to her for a minute, he leaned and kissed her cheek, his beard brushing her skin and his scent lingering with her as he moved away. "You're better than most people I know."

"You are, too."

He laughed and shook his head. "Jenna, you're not seeing things clearly. I'm going to run out and check on the pony. Do you think we should call a veterinarian?"

"I can do it." She stood and followed him to the door, fighting the urge to bite down on her lip, fighting past the pain that her own stubbornness had caused. She should have been more careful. The heat had caused her leg to sweat, irritating skin that was still tender. She knew better. Or at least she was learning.

"I can. You stay here with the boys. I'll come back and give you an update on his condition." He stood at the door. He was Oklahoma again, in jeans and a button-up shirt, the sleeves rolled to his elbows. His hat was pulled low over his eyes. The neatly trimmed goatee framed his smile, making it soft, tender.

"Thank you. Could you tell the boys to come inside?"

Jenna watched the boys run across the lawn with the dog. They had water guns and were shooting each other, soaking their clothes. Water dripped from their hair.

"Sure. You sit down and take it easy." He smiled down at her, and then he touched her hand, his fingers resting against hers.

Jenna nodded, because she couldn't talk, because he was near and she hadn't felt like someone who needed to be kissed in a long time. And he looked like a man about to kiss a woman, like he might be thinking about it, or even fighting it.

"Adam?"

He looked down, leaning a little with one hand on the door frame, and then he let out a sigh. His hand moved to the small of her back, holding her in a way that made her feel safe. He moved a little closer, his head dipping, closer to hers, closer, and then pausing. She thought he might move away. She wanted him to move away. She held her breath, waiting. And then their lips touched.

The kiss was tender, but strong. His hand on her back kept her close. She held on to his arms, needing to be steady, needing to be near him. She needed to feel like a woman a man might want to kiss, even if it only lasted a few seconds.

Thoughts played through her mind and she pushed them back, letting herself feel the moment in his arms, with his lips on hers and his hand on her back. And then she moved away, turning her head a little to break the connection.

Her boys were playing in the yard. Adam Mackenzie was passing through. He wouldn't stay in Dawson, or in her life. They were both temporary for him, this town and her. She made him feel strong. She knew that. And she didn't want to be his strength, not that way, as if she was the weak woman that needed him.

He had brought them dinner. She reminded herself of that fact and so she didn't say something she might regret. There was enough to regret without adding to it.

"I'll go check on the pony." And then he leaned again, kissing her one last time before he walked out the door.

She sat down, watching him go. He was checking on Charlie. And then he was walking back to the house, across the lawn where the boys were playing under one of the big trees that she had played under as a kid. He stopped to talk to them, to her boys. They stood up, showing him what they'd found.

Temporary. He was temporary in their lives. She had to make sure the boys knew, that they understood he wouldn't be in Dawson for long.

"I'm heading out." He stood outside the screen door.

Jenna nodded, but remained in the wheelchair. "I'll see you tomorrow."

"Tomorrow? We're not doing anything at the camp tomorrow."

"Church." She moved closer to the door, not standing up. Standing was suddenly overrated.

"Yes, okay. Do you need a ride?" He looked down. She wished he wouldn't have done that. She wanted to remember the kiss, being held, and not that look.

"Of course I don't."

"Just asking."

"Thanks, but no. I'll be fine." The way she was always fine. She had said those same words to the father of her boys when he left. And she'd said them to Jeff when he left her in the hospital.

"I'll be fine," she repeated with a smile that wavered as he walked away.

At least Adam Mackenzie wasn't making promises that he would break. He wasn't making any promises at all, except one…that he would ultimately leave.

Chapter Nine

Church. Adam hadn't gone in years, not for real. He attended the dedication of Will's daughter. Kaitlin. Today he remembered her name. He pulled into a parking space and cut the engine of the truck. Jenna's truck was already here. He had thought about her last night, and this morning. He had considered calling Clint, because someone should know that she needed help.

He had a feeling she wouldn't thank him for interfering. And then he smiled, because hadn't she been interfering in his life since he showed up in Dawson? Hadn't she given him advice, prodded and pushed him?

She had made him smile more since his arrival than he'd smiled in years. Real smiles. That was the difference.

He got out of the truck, pausing for a minute before walking across the parking lot to the old church with the tall steeple and narrow stained-glass windows. It reminded him of the church he'd grown up in. He didn't want that reminder, of himself as a little boy in Sunday school, listening to Mrs. Pritchard tell him about Jesus. He didn't want to remember bowing his head and praying with her as she introduced him to salvation.

He didn't need a reminder of where he'd come from and how far he'd gone, away from that kid, those roots.

But he couldn't stop remembering. He'd been remembering since he came back here, the memories almost like an open photo album, drawing him back into the images of that childhood, and faith.

"Adam." Clint Cameron walked across the parking lot, no longer the teenager that wanted the same high school girl that Adam had given his class ring to. He smiled at that memory, of the two of them squaring off after a game, and Clint walking away.

Clint hadn't taken football or winning as seriously as Adam. A tinge of envy shot through him, because in the end, Clint had been the winner.

The tall blonde next to him, the baby in her arms. Those two meant more than a champion ring, more than trophies, more than anything he'd accumulated. His life had felt empty for a long time, now the emptiness burrowed deep inside him, pointing out the reasons why.

"Clint. Beautiful morning." But hot. The sun had eaten up the cool of early morning and June heat was already claiming the day. Adam locked his truck door and stepped closer to the couple walking toward him.

"It's supposed to rain later." Careful conversation about weather. "I think you met Willow the other day."

Adam made eye contact with Willow. "Yes, we met."

Adam walked with them up the steps of the church, its tall steeple reaching up. He motioned the couple through the doors of the church ahead of him.

No anonymity here. If he'd gone to church of his own volition, it would have been somewhere big, a place where he could walk in and hide in a back pew. Instead he was here, and people were smiling, waving. A few pointed.

Jenna was sitting on the stage, a guitar in her hands. A country girl in a floral top and jeans, her hair in a ponytail.

Cuter than a speckled pup. His grandfather had used that phrase. He doubted Jenna would appreciate it. But speckled pups were cute. They were easy to take home and keep.

That thought took him by surprise, forcing him to look her way again, to wonder what it was about her that made him think about her at the oddest moments. He'd even thought about her that morning as he drank his coffee and tried to think of reasons not to go to church.

He scooted into the pew next to Clint and he refused to look in the direction of Jenna, even when the music started and he could hear the guitar. She had a gift. She played classical guitar. It shouldn't have surprised him, but it did. She smiled when she caught him looking at her.

By the time Pastor Todd got behind the pulpit, Adam had never been so ready to be preached at. He relaxed a little. But Jenna was walking toward him, leaning a little on the cane. She slid into the pew, into the space next to him. Her arm brushed his.

He didn't think church was the place to remember a kiss, or to think about how good she smelled. It was a good place to think about his life, and leaving Dawson.

But the message was about leaving a person's own ideas and plans behind, and finding the path God has for them. Adam pretended the message wasn't for him. He tried not to think about what had brought him here, each incident or coincidence.

Coincidence. It was all a fluke—this camp, Billy, her boys in the road. Her. It wasn't about his life changing or a new direction. He was here to get a camp started. He had a job interview in a few weeks.

His life wasn't about Oklahoma.

* * *

Jenna felt as if she had held her breath through the entire service. Of course she hadn't, or she would have passed out. And then she thought about what a relief passing out would have been, if it had meant not being aware of Adam Mackenzie sitting next to her. He took up too much space.

With the closing prayer, she stood, ready to escape. Willow stopped her retreat.

"Lunch at our house?" Willow's tone was soft, the baby she held cooing against her shoulder, wrapping tiny fingers through blond hair.

Jenna had never been jealous of her brother and his wife, but at moments like this, she wanted what they had. She wanted to be a part of a couple that met their challenges together.

The man next to her moved, trying to slide past her. She stepped back, but Willow spoke again.

"Adam, why don't you join us? The Mad Cow is closed on Sunday, and Clint is grilling burgers."

"I am?" Clint gathered the diaper bag, his wife's purse, and Jenna thought she saw him gather his wits. "Of course I am."

"I shouldn't. I have..." Adam looked like he was searching for a good excuse. Jenna knew, because she was busy trying to think of something she needed to be doing. Scrubbing toilets seemed preferable to this.

"You should." Willow patted his arm. "Come on, we can use help. Clint always burns burgers on the grill."

Adam looked from Jenna to Willow and then he accepted, that easily. And Jenna wanted him to find his own excuse, his own reason that he couldn't go, because this should have been her safe time, in a safe place. She wanted to find a corner and hide.

Instead she met her brother's concerned gaze, his half smile, his wink. Clint understood. There were times when she wanted privacy, not curious stares and questions.

But she didn't have time to dwell on it. The boys would be waiting for her to check them out of children's church.

"I need to get Timmy and David." She walked away, leaving them to make their plans.

"Mom." Timmy ran out of the classroom to greet her as she walked down the hall to the room that was a dining area part of the time, and a classroom the rest of the time.

"Hey, sweetie. Get your brother, okay." She leaned against the door, taking weight off her left leg. If this kept up, she wouldn't be able to use her prosthesis until the sores healed. She had to give herself a break.

She didn't know how to take breaks. She didn't want to stop living her life, or stop being a mom. She had so much to do.

And now she had to face lunch with Adam invading her family.

She picked up the pen and signed the boys out. One of the workers gave her a sympathetic smile.

"Doing okay, Jenna?"

"I am, just tired."

"It's a good day for a nap," the woman encouraged. "Maybe the boys will take one, too."

"Look what we made!" David held up a scroll with the Ten Commandments written in his childish handwriting. He was bouncing and had a red juice drink mustache. She doubted the nap idea.

"Wow, that is pretty neat." She took it from him, and smiled. Thou Shalt Not Convict. She was sure he meant *covet*.

"Isn't it great? We learned the commandments." Timmy handed her his scroll.

"Very good, guys. Those are important rules to remember."

"We're not going to kill or steal, Mom." David took his scroll back. "But I don't even understand all those other ones."

"You'll understand them better as you get older. Some of them are about jealousy. Jealousy is when you want what someone else has. We're supposed to be content with the good things we already have."

The good things.

Hadn't she just battled her own jealous feelings? Clint and Willow deserved their happiness. And even happiness had its moments of regret, failure or trials. Clint and Willow had battled to get where they were. They still had some battles to face as Willow's hearing loss progressed.

She knew that it was easy to look in from the outside and think that someone else had a perfect life. She knew no one had a perfect life.

She followed along behind the boys. And at the door, Clint and Willow were waiting with Adam. He unbuttoned the top two buttons of the deep blue shirt he was wearing and pulled at his collar. She almost felt sorry for him. Almost.

Instead she smiled and laughed a little. "It wasn't so bad, was it?"

"What?"

"Church?" She pulled her keys out of her pocket. Carrying a purse was sometimes too much. She had her driver's license in her pocket, too.

"It was good. I didn't realize you played guitar."

"Classical lessons from a music teacher in school. She thought I had promise, but lacked direction." She shaded her eyes against the sun as she looked up at him.

"Really?"

She laughed. "Yes, really. I was a little on the wild side back then."

"I can't imagine."

"You don't need to. Just take my word for it. Come on, boys." She herded them across the parking lot toward her truck. "See you at Clint's."

As they drove, she noticed a car pull in behind Adam's truck. It followed them through town, turned when they turned and followed them to the drive that led to Clint's. Jenna kept her eyes on the road in front of her, but occasionally flicked her attention to the rearview mirror and that car. She could see Adam's face in her mirror, could see the way he watched his own mirror.

Jenna pulled into the drive next to the log home that had once been Janie's, but was now Clint's and Willow's. A baby swing sat on the front porch next to the swing and rocking chairs. Life had changed a lot in one year.

A year. The boys climbed out of the truck, exiting through the passenger's side door. They wanted to see Willow's dog and the llama that Clint had bought at an auction. Now the boys were begging her to get one of the silly creatures.

One year. She had left the boys here one year ago, with Clint, Willow and Janie. She had returned six months later, her entire life and her future completely changed. She had returned to be a single mom, without an engagement ring on her finger, and with new challenges to face. This challenge would never go away.

She had returned with something new. She had returned with faith. She knew she could make it through anything. She'd already been tested, and she'd survived.

She eased out of the truck, always a reminder of

how things had changed. There were new ways of doing everything. The things she'd always taken for granted were now appreciated. Walking wasn't taken for granted.

There were days, like today, when she knew that she couldn't do what she wanted to do. She couldn't run after her boys. She couldn't climb a fence or get on a horse. Not today, but tomorrow, if she took care of herself.

She made it to the front porch and sat down on the swing. Adam had gotten out of his truck and he was walking up to the car that had followed him. A woman got out. The woman, a brunette, stared at Adam, wiping her eyes as she took a few steps toward him.

Jenna got up and went inside.

"Elizabeth." Adam approached his older sister. He hadn't seen her in a few years. Seeing her now, he realized what a mistake that had been.

"Creep." She had always called him that. Sometimes she had said it with a smile, and sometimes she had meant the word.

He smiled. "Good to see you, too."

She wiped at her eyes. "No, I mean it this time. You could visit your family."

"Yeah, I know."

Adam leaned back against her car and pulled sunglasses out of his pocket because he'd left his hat in the truck. He slipped them on and Elizabeth moved to stand next to him. She hadn't changed a lot. She still knew how to put him in his place. She had never been his biggest fan.

"You could have come to see us. Or invited us up to see you."

"I didn't think you'd be interested."

"Really? You thought that?" She let out an exasperated sigh. "You're my brother."

"Yes, I am." He wondered if she had forgotten the rift that had grown between them, and how it had happened. "You made this rule, Elizabeth. I just honored it."

"You took the easy way out."

"*'I'm so sick of you being the star, Adam. I'm in this family, too, but when was the last time anyone noticed me?'*" He repeated her words, because he'd never forgotten them, or the stark pain on her face when she said them.

Or how it had hurt him to hear that from her, to know how much she resented him. He had envied her, she had resented him. What a crazy way to grow up.

"I was eighteen, going away to college and Dad wasn't going to drive me to Oklahoma City because you had a game." She turned to look at him, and the pain was still there in her eyes.

"I know. But I didn't ask him to be that way. I didn't want it to be that way."

"We let this happen, didn't we?" She started walking toward the barn. Adam walked next to her, not sure what to say.

They crossed the road and she walked up to the metal pole fence that held Willow's bulls. She stood close, finding a shady spot beneath an oak tree. He stopped next to her.

"We're brother and sister. That should mean something. We should spend holidays together. You should call me when you're in town. Those are the things families normally do."

He had to agree because he knew from watching other people, from watching Clint and Jenna, that families should share their lives. They hadn't learned to do that in their family. His family had been about football. Elizabeth had stayed at home, reading.

"You're right." He really didn't know her. She sent pictures each year of the kids, and of their Christmas. They had an occasional holiday together. But he didn't know her, or her family.

"Of course I'm right." She touched his arm. "I'm also sorry. Really sorry."

"I'm sorry, too."

"Whose place is this?" Elizabeth looked from the barn to the house.

"Clint Cameron's." He glanced back at the house. Jenna had gone inside. "I was jealous of you, too."

"Why?"

"You had freedom." Adam felt childish making that statement. The thoughts of a teenager weren't easy on the lips of a man.

"I wasn't the star of the family."

"I would have given you that place. I didn't ask to be the star of the show."

She closed her eyes. "You know, I played the flute in band. Dad never came to a parade, a concert, not once did he acknowledge my achievements from the pulpit like he did yours. He was all about you."

"I guess I didn't see all of that." He slid an arm around her shoulder and pulled her close. "I didn't have time to really look at what was going on in our family. I slept, ate and played football. If I wasn't playing, I was practicing. Winning wasn't enough for him."

"He wanted to be you. He wanted to be the champion. You were the way for him to be that person."

"But I didn't want it as much as he wanted it. He could taste it."

"Why did you keep playing?"

"I didn't know how to stop. I didn't want to disappoint him."

Adam Mackenzie hated football. Not the game, but what it had been in his home, his life. There were times that he loved to play. He loved victory. He loved that it had gotten him out of Oklahoma.

And now he was back. His sister was standing next to him, and the past had become the present.

Adam stared out at the bulls grazing in the pen, trying to decide if he was happy with the change of events. His sister in his life, not wanting something, just wanting his niece and nephews to know him. She shouldn't have to ask him for that.

"It shouldn't be a difficult thing for you, having a family," she half teased, but the expression on her face questioned him.

"It isn't difficult, just new territory." He turned his back on the fence, and they started back toward the house, crossing the gravel drive and being greeted by a blue heeler. "You should bring your family to the camp while I'm here."

"This camp, is this what Billy was doing?"

"It is."

"Now you're doing it?" She walked next to him.

"Not really. I'm taking care of what was already started. This isn't my thing, or where I want to be."

They were almost at the house, a long, ranch-style home, the covered porch running its entire length. The front door opened and Jenna walked out. She had stars in her eyes, but she didn't know him. Not really.

He wondered if he even knew himself.

"Clint has burgers on the grill." Jenna focused on the woman standing next to Adam. She could see the resemblance between the two and knew that it was the sister she had spoken to. "You can eat with us, if you like."

"I should go."

"There's plenty." Jenna ignored the warning look in Adam's eyes, telling her to stay out of his business.

"No, really, I have a family waiting for me." She stood on tiptoe and kissed Adam's cheek. "Call me. I know you have my number in your phone."

"I do." He hugged her. "We'll talk soon."

"For real this time." Elizabeth walked away.

Jenna walked down the steps and stood next to Adam. He needed a friend. She could be that for him. She wondered if he even knew what it was, to have a real friend.

"The boys found a football in the garage. They want to know if you'll play with them."

"There are better things to do with their time." He turned and walked into the house, leaving her on the steps, watching his sister drive away.

"Okay, maybe we won't play football," she muttered to herself as she followed him into the house. He didn't even know where he was going.

He was waiting in the kitchen.

"Through the dining room and out the French doors." She pointed. "I'll be out in a minute."

"What are you doing?" He didn't leave.

She sat down at the kitchen table, not knowing what to say. And this was why she hadn't wanted him here. "I have to rest."

"You can't do that outside?"

Of course he wasn't making this easy for her. She looked down, avoiding his deep blue eyes.

"I have to take the prosthesis off. I'm still gaining

strength in my muscles, but some days are difficult." She said it with as matter-of-fact a tone as she could master, keeping emotion out of it, making it easier to look up, meeting his steady gaze. And then she saw tenderness in his eyes.

She felt heat work its way up her neck into her cheeks. This was not the way to feel beautiful, like someone a man would want to hold. She wasn't whole. She would never be whole.

Adam was still standing in front of her.

"What can I do?" He kneeled in front of her, a big giant, suddenly at her level. She wanted to touch his cheek.

Worse, she wanted someone to hold her.

Man, she really thought she was past that. She had worked hard at convincing herself that she was good at being alone. She had the boys. She had her career. And now this guy had blown into her life to upset her plans about making it on her own.

It was something that would pass. Of course it would. At this point, any man probably would have caused this weak moment.

"Jenna?"

"Tell me what your sister wanted. You can take my mind off what must be pretty red cheeks and a lot of in-security by sharing your family drama." It was easier to laugh than to cry. It gave her a moment to remind herself that she was a whole person. "I'm really nosy, if you hadn't noticed."

"She wants to fix our relationship." He shrugged. "It's probably about time."

"Oh." Jenna hadn't expected an answer, just a momentary distraction, maybe an argument or a "none of your business."

"And she told me to visit my dad."

"Why?"

"None of your business." That was more like it, and it made her smile. "Come on, let's get you back to the party, Cinderella."

"What?"

"Do what you need to do, and I'll carry you outside."

"You can't carry me around." The heat that had vanished returned to her cheeks. "I have crutches, in the hall closet."

"I really can carry you." He stood and flexed his biceps.

"So, you'll carry me outside and leave me?"

"No, I won't do that."

But he would. She knew that he wasn't even with her at that moment. She could see in his eyes that he'd detached. Maybe to deal with her, maybe to deal with his own pain.

She pulled up her pant leg and removed the prosthesis. Adam watched. She pointed to the hall, distracting him, taking his careful gaze off her. "Closet, crutches."

He nodded and obeyed. When he returned, he held them out to her and reached for her hand. She pulled up, situating herself and getting her balance.

"This is embarrassing," she whispered as heat crawled up her neck into her cheeks.

"Don't. You really don't have to worry about me."

"I'm sure it isn't the relationship you thought we'd have when you crashed into my ditch."

"It isn't. I thought I'd drive into town, square the camp away and be gone." He brushed her cheek with the back of his hand and it rested there. "I hadn't expected to find a friend."

"We should go outside." She moved, turning to head

out the back door. Adam whispered something about her being a chicken. She walked through the door pretending she hadn't heard. She knew what she was. She also knew how to protect herself.

Chapter Ten

Adam watched as she settled herself in a lawn chair under an umbrella. Jenna Cameron, Clint's little sister. He was glad when she seemed ready to be on her own, meaning conversation with him wasn't necessary. That was fine, he would rather it be that way. He didn't want to be the person that hurt Clint's little sister.

Adam walked to the grill and Clint. Willow was watching the grill, a spray bottle of water in hand.

"Is that in case he starts a fire?" Adam smiled as he said the words and Willow nodded.

"He's not a good grill man."

"Could I help?"

Willow glanced past him. "No, that's okay. You can relax. We've got it handled. Lunch will be ready in five minutes."

"Are we going to eat out here?"

"We'll eat on the deck. The fan keeps it a little cooler." Clint turned, nodding to a covered area with a table.

Willow touched his arm when he glanced Jenna's way again. "She's fine."

"Oh, I know she is." But he wasn't convinced.

"Adam, play with us." Timmy ran across the yard, a football in his little hands. Adam shook his head. "Let's play something else, guys. How about tag? I'll be it."

"No, football." David had joined them. David, who never pushed.

"What if…"

"Guys, leave Adam alone. He's on vacation from football." Jenna gave the twins a warning look. They nodded and ran off, still carrying the football.

And dreaming of being him. He knew that's what boys did. They wanted to be in the big leagues. He hadn't known what else to be. He hadn't been allowed to dream of anything else.

The boys tossed the football to one another, fumbling it, not getting it across the lawn. They didn't have a dad to teach them the right way to pass. He looked back at Clint.

They had an uncle who could do that for them.

A scream stopped Adam from walking away. He turned and David was standing in the middle of the lawn, a hand on his cheek and the football bouncing across the ground in front of him.

Jenna scrambled to get up. "What happened?"

"Timmy threw it hard." David rubbed at his face, the way a boy did when it hurt and he didn't want to cry. Adam knew that trick.

He also knew that sinking feeling of needing to do something. Jenna started to get up. He raised his hand to stop her. And this wasn't what he had planned, this much involvement in their lives.

"Here, buddy, let me see." Adam crossed the yard and David met him halfway. Adam kneeled down, putting himself at the child's level. "Take your hand down."

David rubbed again and then moved his hand. He shot a gaze past Adam, to Jenna. He wanted his mom.

Adam could imagine that he was a poor second to Jenna. Out of the corner of his eye he could see her perched on the edge of the chair.

"You're going to have a shiner. That makes you a man. A real football player." Adam touched the skin that was already starting to bruise. "You sit by your mom and I'll get something to put on this."

"Steak?" Timmy was standing behind Adam, looking over his shoulder at the brother he'd injured. And he was jealous, Adam could hear it in his tone, as if steak on a black eye was the best thing in the world.

"No, not steak." Adam put a hand on David's slim shoulder. "A bag of frozen peas."

"They use steak in the movies," Timmy offered.

"I know, but frozen peas work and they're less messy." Adam stood. "Come on, let's go see your mom and I'll see if Willow has a bag of frozen peas."

David stuck a hand in his. The gesture shouldn't have been more than a guy could take, like that hand in his meant something. He'd never felt stronger in his life.

Jenna looked at them, at their hands joined, and then her face tilted, and her eyes met his, questioning him. Or maybe warning him. Yes, definitely a warning. Because he would be leaving soon, and the boys wouldn't understand. He led David to her and when her arms opened, the child flew into them, no longer the tough guy that rubbed away his tears.

Toughen up, be a man. Adam remembered his dad's words when he'd gotten hurt on the football field. His mom had never been the soft touch. She had wanted the dream almost as much as his dad. She had cheered from the sidelines, yelling when she thought the ref was wrong about a play, yelling at him to do better.

His success had taken them places.

Toughen up. He shook off pain that hadn't left a scar or a bruise on his body.

"Adam?"

He shook it off and smiled at the woman waiting for him to respond.

"I'll get that bag of peas." He touched David's head, and the little boy looked up, his eye squinting. A little hand quickly rubbed away the tears. "Let me take a closer look. You know, David, it's okay to cry."

David nodded and a tear slid down his cheek. He brushed it away. "I know."

"I'll be right back."

Or maybe he should get in his truck and start driving, as far from this family as he could get. It might be safer to be with his parents than to be here with Jenna and her boys.

It would feel a lot safer back in Atlanta, in his world, his life. He knew what to expect from the people in that life and what to expect from himself when he was around them.

Jenna held David against her, his tiny arms wrapped around her neck. "You stink," she whispered.

She snuggled against him and he snuggled back, a sweaty little boy who needed a bath. He climbed onto her lap, keeping his arms around her. Timmy climbed up next to her, not wanting to be left out, and biting his lip the way he did when he felt guilty.

"Be more careful next time, guys." She slipped an arm around Timmy and pulled him to her side.

"Are you okay, David?" Willow squatted in front of them. She had the bag of peas that Adam had recommended and she placed them on David's eye and cheek. "That's quite a bruise."

He smiled big. "I know. That's pretty neat, huh?"

"Yeah, pretty neat." Willow kissed the top of his head. "And you are really sweaty. Do you want them to wash their hands before we eat lunch?"

Jenna nodded. "And I need to get up and help you get the table set."

"No, you don't. Come on, Jenna, take a break. It really is okay. I bet Timmy can help me." Willow stood and reached a hand for Timmy to take.

"I like to help," Timmy assured Jenna, kissing her on the cheek. "Adam can take care of you and David. He's pretty good at that."

Jenna felt that heat again, and she realized it was becoming a pretty common event. And then another thought hit her, dispelling the warmth in her cheeks and leaving her cold. Was Timmy feeling the burden of taking care of his mom? The thought sunk to the pit of her stomach and rested there.

She watched Timmy and Willow walk away and then a shadow loomed, blocking the sun. She glanced up, into the darkened profile of Adam Mackenzie. She didn't want to face him, especially if he'd heard her son's proclamation that Adam was good at taking care of her.

Poor guy, he'd gotten more than he'd bargained for when he showed up in Dawson.

"Ready to eat?"

"I'm ready." She pushed herself up and maneuvered across the yard to the table. One hop up and then she could sit. Adam stood nearby, watching. "You can relax, I'm not going to fall or break."

"I know that."

She sat down and David took the seat next to hers. The fan pushed the air, cooling it to bearable. At least there were clouds floating over, sometimes blocking the sun. And maybe later there would be rain. At times she thought she could smell it in the air, a promise of moisture and cooler air.

Clint walked across the yard with the plate of burgers and set them on the table. They were barely burned. She smiled up at him and his eyes narrowed.

"Don't even say it." He handed her two plates.

"I only wanted to say thank you, nothing else. Don't be so touchy."

He laughed, her cowboy brother, dressed for church. Willow had taught him how to match his clothes. "Right, you were going to say thank you."

"I was." She smiled up at him, loving him. He had always been there for her. "And I was going to follow that by saying you're doing so much better. Remember when you asked me if cookies were a breakfast food?"

"I do remember, and for some reason you didn't approve."

"I thought there were better things for the boys. But you were there for them."

"See, I did something right."

She reached for his hand. "You did a lot of things right."

The door slid open. Adam walked out carrying the salad bowl. Jenna released her brother's hand and took the bowl from Adam. He didn't look at her, didn't seem to notice that their fingers touched, and the connection made breathing difficult. For her, not him. Okay, that was fine, she could play that game. When he walked back into the house, Clint sat down in the seat at the end of the table.

"Don't take it personally." He shrugged. "I don't think he's good at relationships."

"Stop reading tabloids." Jenna poured tea in her glass. "And his ability to handle relationships isn't any of my business. But I do like it when people make eye contact with me, rather than acting like avoiding me will make it easier to avoid what happened."

"Okay, you win." Clint stood up. "I'm going to see if Willow needs anything, and then I'm going to get my baby girl."

"She's beautiful."

"Yeah, she is."

The door opened again. Willow handed Clint the ketchup and mustard. He took them. "Do you want me to get Lindsey?"

She shook her head. "She's still sleeping. I have the monitor on."

Disappointment flashed across Clint's features and Willow smiled. "Clint, she needs to sleep. You can't keep waking her up."

"Yeah, yeah." He signed something and Willow turned pink.

"Not fair." Jenna laughed, because she had started learning sign language, but Clint and Willow were speed talkers compared to Jenna's weak attempts.

"Private conversation." Clint winked and kissed his wife before walking back into the house, making room at the door for Adam.

"Adam, sit down." Willow pointed to the seat that Clint had vacated. The one next to Jenna. He sat down and then he looked at Jenna.

"Do you need anything?" he asked, his attention focused past her, to David. Still no eye contact.

I need for you to look at me. She didn't say it. She wouldn't. He was being kind. He wanted to be helpful. "No, I don't need anything. Do you?"

He grinned, that half smile touched with a boyish charm, and this time their eyes connected. "No, I think I'm fine."

"Good, because you were starting to get on my nerves."

"What?"

"Acting all sorry, and like I'm something breakable that needs to be kept on a shelf. Adam, I train horses for a living. I live on a farm. I'm having a rough couple of days, a setback, but I'm not broken."

"I know." His eyes met hers and held her gaze. "I do know that you're strong. I'm sorry."

"Good, as long as we have that settled, let's get the two love birds out here so we can eat. I'm starving."

The door opened and Timmy walked out of the house, shaking his head. He grinned. "Uncle Clint is kissing Aunt Willow. That's gross."

Jenna gave a fake shudder. "Ewww, gross."

But she remembered what it felt like to be held in Adam Mackenzie's arms. She remembered what it felt like to want to linger there, in a kiss.

She remembered feeling beautiful.

Adam left after lunch. He'd offered Jenna a ride home, but she had insisted that the afternoon rest would have her back on her feet by tomorrow and he didn't have to stay. Willow had even refused his help with the dishes.

So he got into his truck and drove away, away from the farm, away from a ton of conflicting emotions. Because he hadn't been ready to leave a Sunday afternoon with people he liked, and he had known it was time to go.

He drove past the entrance to Camp Hope, the sign now up and the driveway widened and the weeds mowed so it could be seen. Camp would start tomorrow. And then what?

He didn't know, because this hadn't been a part of his plan. He hadn't expected to stay here. He sure couldn't have guessed that Will would discover that the accounts had been cleaned out.

If he left, what would people say? Probably not much. Staying was more of a surprise to people than his leaving would be. The world probably expected him to bail on the camp, on the kids. He was Adam Mackenzie, he didn't think about other people.

Wouldn't they be surprised if they knew that he couldn't stop thinking about Jenna Cameron? The reality of that surprised him more than a little.

He replaced thoughts of her with thoughts of his dad, and the home he'd grown up in. He kept driving. Thirty minutes later he was slowing down in front of that house, a white stucco, set back from the road and flanked by a barn. He drove past it, going the few miles to the church where his father had been the pastor.

Those people had loved his dad, really loved him.

What had Adam been missing? Or maybe it wasn't what he was missing, but what he knew. His dad wasn't perfect. His dad had pushed Adam, and then pushed him more, insisting that he be the best. Even at church Adam had been set apart, by his dad, by teachers. The pastor's son, the football star, the charming kid who had gotten away with too much.

He slowed in front of the church and pulled in the driveway. His dad was still pastor here. Twenty-five years of being the pastor of the same church, the same group of people. Twenty-five years of preaching a message that Adam had accepted as a child, and then he'd walked away. Because he'd gotten tired of trying to be perfect.

And now, when he didn't know what to do next, he was here, trying to find direction for his life. He parked his truck and got out, remembering a childhood in this building, being taught by ladies who had hugged him tight and fed him cookies.

Memories he shouldn't have forgotten had returned. He remembered playing baseball in the field behind the church and his dad cheering him on.

A car pulled in the driveway. The automobile was familiar; Adam had seen pictures after he'd sent the check that purchased it from a dealer in Tulsa. He watched his dad pull into the designated parking space and get out, a little older, a little less hair.

"Son."

Adam took a few steps to separate the distance between them.

"Dad, I didn't expect to see you here."

"No, I guess you didn't. I came down to make sure the air conditioner is on for this evening's service. You going to stay?"

"No, I have to get back to Dawson."

"Yes, I heard you've been there." The older Mackenzie rubbed the bald area of his forehead. He pulled off wire-framed glasses and cleaned them with the tail of his shirt. "We thought you might come by the house."

"I've been planning on it." Which wasn't a lie. He had planned on seeing them at least once before he left.

"Adam, life is too short to go on this way." His dad looked away. "I've done funerals lately, burying people that were my friends. It makes a man think about what he's missed out on."

"Yeah, that does make a guy think."

Adam pushed his hat back on his head and made eye contact with an older version of himself. Except the hair. His dad had started balding in his twenties. It was genetic, just like the two of them always believing they were right was genetic. That was the trait they shared.

They'd been butting heads since Adam learned to walk, his mom said. Adam had been the kid that if his dad said it was snowing, Adam would insist it was rain. And when it came to football, sometimes the teenaged Adam had stopped trying because he knew that no matter what, his dad would push him when they got home, push him to rethink, to replay, and to do better.

"Boy, it's hot out here."

"Yeah, it is." Adam walked up the sidewalk and sat down on the steps that led to the front entrance of the church. His dad followed. The church sat on the edge of town, surrounded by farmland.

"How's the camp going?" His dad sat down next to him.

"I hope it's good. The first group of campers shows up tomorrow."

"Are you going to stay and run this thing?"

"No, you know I'm not qualified for that. I'm just the lucky guy that inherited this mess."

"It isn't such a mess. Billy meant well."

"I know he did." A normal conversation. Adam sighed and tipped his hat a little lower. "It really is hot out here."

"Yeah, you're just not as tough as you used to be. You used to practice for hours in weather like this."

"Not my best memories, Dad."

"I know. Adam, I'm sorry if I pushed you too hard. Your sister and I have talked about this. I don't know why I didn't see. She said we never took a family vacation. I guess I thought football was what our family did together."

"Yeah, I know." Adam glanced sideways, shrugging a little, trying to brush it off.

He had meant to come home, put the camp up for sale and leave. Instead it was turning into a bad episode of *Dr. Phil*, and everyone was feeling better but him.

Because he wondered how it would feel to leave, and at one time he could think of nothing but leaving.

"It wasn't such a bad life, was it?" His dad stared out the parking lot, but he shot Adam a quick look. "I mean, look at where you got."

"It got me where I am. But sometimes I wonder where I'd be if it had been my choice. If you hadn't pushed, where would I have gone and what would I have been?"

"I pushed you because I knew you wouldn't push yourself."

"So what? What if I hadn't pushed myself? What if I hadn't succeeded in football? Maybe I could have made decisions about my life, my future." Maybe he wouldn't resent his father, if it had been about something more than success.

"What would you have picked, Adam?"

"I don't know, Dad. Maybe I would have been…" A fireman? He smiled, because every boy probably wanted to be a fireman. "I don't know what I would have done. But I don't think I would have been a failure."

"You can still make decisions for yourself. I pushed you and now you have opportunities you wouldn't have had."

"Yeah, I guess." But he could only remember nights with floodlights on in the backyard, running drills as his dad yelled, coaching him to do better, to not give up.

And he remembered two little boys playing football in the backyard, thinking it was the greatest thing in the world. And he hadn't tossed the football for them, hadn't shown them a better way, because he didn't want to take away the fun of just playing, of being boys.

He should have played with them. Next time—if there was a next time—he would.

"I need to go." He stood and his dad pushed himself

up, nearly Adam's height, not quite. A long time ago Adam had thought his dad was a giant. "Tell Mom I'll stop by the house in a few days."

"She'd like to see you. We both would."

"Maybe we can have a family dinner, with Elizabeth and her family."

"That would be good." His dad crossed the parking lot at his side. "Adam, I hope someday you'll forgive me."

Adam stopped walking. "It isn't about forgiving you, Dad. I think it's about trying to understand you. I'd like for us—would have liked for us—to have a relationship that included something other than football." He pulled his keys out of his pocket. "I would have liked to have gone fishing, or camping."

"I get that." His dad stepped back as Adam opened his truck door. "I'll see you soon. Maybe I'll come down and take a look at that camp."

Adam nodded and shifted into Reverse. "That would be good."

Chapter Eleven

Adam drove for hours after leaving his dad. The sun was setting when he drove back to Dawson and turned on the road that led to his temporary home. He slowed as he passed Jenna's drive on the way back to Camp Hope. The little farmhouse, white siding and covered front porch, was aglow with lights. He could see the dog on the front porch and a shadow as one of the boys walked in front of the window.

He stopped and backed up to turn into her drive, rather than going on up the road to the drive that led to his new home, a single-wide trailer at the edge of a field. What would his friends think of this new life, of Jenna?

When he stopped in the driveway next to her house, the dog got up and barked, but then his tail wagged and he ran down to greet Adam.

He hadn't had a pet in years. Morgan's son, Rob, had had a kitten that they picked up in a parking lot, a stray with greasy gray fur and big ears. Rob had loved that kitten. Adam had really cared about Rob. Too bad Morgan had only wanted invitations to certain parties, and then she'd dumped him.

He didn't get out of his truck, because a single mom was inside that house and she had two boys who needed a dad. That was the talk around town. He'd overheard it in the grocery store, what a pair the two of them would be. How Jenna needed someone like him.

He'd had a lifetime of being used.

The front door opened and Jenna stepped out, still on crutches, looking smaller than ever, and fragile. But she wasn't.

She moved to the edge of the porch but didn't come down the ramp. He lowered his window. "I was driving by."

"It looks to me like you stopped driving. Driving by would mean going on down the road, not stopping."

He smiled. "Yeah, you got me there. Do you have iced tea?"

"I'm from Oklahoma, of course I have iced tea. The boys are getting into the tub. Do you want to come in, or are you going to stay in your truck?"

"I'll get out." The dog met him, tail wagging. He reached down to ruffle the thick fur around his neck and then the dog followed him to the house.

"Come in. Let me check on their bathwater, and you put ice in the glasses."

As if he'd always been here, always been in her world.

He walked through the living room, aware of his boots on the hardwood floor that glowed like warm honey. The house was small but, man, it made him feel at home. It was the kind of place a guy didn't want to leave.

This house had overstuffed furniture with throw pillows embroidered by hand, curtains that lifted in the early-evening breeze, and candles that scented the air with the aroma of baked apples. It also had two boys who needed a dad. And he wasn't the best candidate for that job.

He opened the freezer and pulled out ice cube trays, listening as Jenna talked to the boys about how to wash, and then told them that if they made a mess, they had to clean it up. Her voice was soft with laughter and the twins jabbered nonstop.

The sounds were as foreign to him as Atlanta had once been, and yet, somehow it was all familiar, as if it had always been a part of his life.

Warning signs were going off, telling him to retreat, to get out of her world before he got pulled into something that hurt them all. But he couldn't walk away.

Jenna walked into the kitchen as he was filling up two glasses and she pulled a container out of the cabinet. "Willow made chocolate chip cookies. Want one?"

"Can I have two?"

"Have as many as you want." She took two and nodded to the table. "We can sit in here. Or on the porch."

"The porch would be great." Without asking, he grabbed her tea. She smiled and didn't protest.

He followed her out the door onto the small porch with the two metal chairs and a swing. Lamplight glowed from the living room and he could hear the boys playing in the bathroom, just off the living room.

"I love nights like this." Jenna sat down and reached for her glass. "I love it here."

"It is a good place," he admitted. He looked out at the lawn, at the sky that had turned deep twilight-blue. The stars were amazing, maybe because he hadn't seen them like this in so many years. In Atlanta, he never looked up.

"Where'd you go today?" She sighed. "Sorry, that's none of my business."

He smiled at her. "I went home. I saw my dad."

"Good. A guy should always be able to go home." She made it sound so easy.

He wished it was. Maybe it was, for other people. He had come to the conclusion that the water under the bridge had washed him downstream a little too far, taking him too far from his family, too far from where he'd grown up. And too far from faith.

Now none of it felt as far away as he'd once thought.

"Are you always such an optimist?" he asked, but he already knew the answer.

"Not always. I know what it's like to have to forgive someone. I had to forgive my dad for hurting me, for hurting us, and for spending so much of my childhood drunk."

"I'm sorry, Jenna."

"I've worked through it. He's in the nursing home now, suffering from dementia. Sometimes he doesn't even know who I am. The past doesn't seem as important as it used to."

"Yeah, my dad told me that he's had to do the funerals of friends his age. It does make you stop and think. I also realize I've spent too many years angry with him for pushing me the way he did."

"You would have played anyway." She smiled in the dim light on the porch, and her hand moved, like she meant to reach for his, but she didn't. "You could have walked away. You went to college. If you hadn't wanted this…"

"I could have done something else." He laughed a little, because she never gave him any slack. "You're right, I guess I could have. And now I *am* going to do something else. The job with the sports network."

"See, doors opened because your dad pushed you."

"Yes, he pushed." Adam leaned back, thinking about those ladies and their whispered comments about the two of them. "Jenna, I'm not a good person."

"Have you been reading too many stories about your-self and believing what other people say?" She winked, teasing with her smile.

"Don't you believe those stories?"

"No, I don't believe them. I think you've done things you regret. But I don't believe that's who you are." She cocked her head to the side and he didn't talk. He knew she was listening to her boys. They were still chatter-ing, still splashing in the tub.

"The kids show up tomorrow for the first day of Camp Hope."

"I know." She shifted in the chair. "I might not be around for a day or two. I need to take some time with my horses."

"You don't have to explain that to me. I know you have a life."

"I'm not explaining." She laughed a little. "Okay, maybe I am. But the horses are important to me. When I was little, this is what I dreamed of."

"Didn't you have other dreams?" He turned in his chair, watching her in the soft light that glowed from the living room window.

She sighed a little. "I wanted to run away from home. I wanted to show horses on the national circuit and never come back to Dawson. Kind of like you. But my dream changed. Now it's about this farm and raising my boys. What was your dream?"

His dream? The likely answer, the one he'd always given to reporters, was that he'd always wanted to play pro football. But there had to be other dreams, other things he wanted in life. He smiled, not looking at her, because he knew what she'd think.

"I wanted to be a fireman."

Her laughter filled the night air. "Of course you did.

Every little boy wants to be a fireman. But what else? What did you really want to be?"

"I'm serious. I wanted to be a fireman."

"So, volunteer for the Dawson Rural Fire District. They can always use help."

"I won't be here long enough." The words plunked into the night, having the opposite effect of her laughter. He wouldn't be here long at all.

"No, I guess you won't."

He glanced at his watch, and then out at the dark sky. No streetlights, no traffic, no sirens. He had forgotten that this type of silence existed. He had forgotten, or maybe never known, what it was like to sit and talk to a woman like Jenna Cameron.

"I should go home."

She stood when he stood. "Yes, it is getting late."

And her smile was gone, and he knew that it was because he was leaving. Did she wonder if he would sell the camp? He wished he had an answer for her.

He picked up both their glasses. "I'll take these in first."

"Thank you."

Jenna didn't follow Adam into the house. She could hear the boys playing in the bath, fighting with toy men and splashing water, probably all over the floor. Adam came back, his face in shadows with the living room light behind him. She waited on the porch to tell him goodbye.

He stepped onto the porch and the dog came up, rolling over in front of Adam so he could scratch its belly. Adam gave the dog the attention it wanted and then straightened, reaching for his hat that he'd left on the table.

Jenna knew that he should go. For her sake and for

the boys'. They didn't need to get attached to him, or get used to him in their lives.

Adam still stood on her porch, though. He smelled like mountains and cedar. And when he was this close, she could hardly breathe.

She needed to breathe.

She took a step back, taking in a deep breath of humid June air. Adam backed up a step in the other direction. He had to know as well as she did that this—whatever *this* was—couldn't be real. It was moonlight and missing something they'd never had, would never have. She had two kids. He had career plans that included Atlanta, not Dawson.

"Adam, you should go now."

She had a list of reasons why he should go. She had a five-year plan that didn't include dating. Her boys were in the bathroom splashing, playing and needing for her to be there for them.

If she closed her eyes she could remember how it felt when Jeff looked at her that day that he said goodbye. She could remember how his gaze had lingered on her leg. She would never open herself up that way again, to feel that way, with a man looking at her as if she was less than beautiful.

She was past the anger, past the hurt. She had worked through so many stages of grief. She couldn't remember them all, but she knew that it had left something raw and painful inside her, an unwillingness to ever be hurt that way again.

"I'll see you tomorrow. Or in a few days." Adam's voice, reminding her of this night, and her life here.

She opened her eyes and nodded. "I'll be around."

"Okay then." He didn't walk away. "Jenna, people are talking about us."

"Oh?" What was she supposed to say? "I haven't heard, but I can imagine."

"It's just that I know how you feel, about the boys."

"Don't worry, I know you're going back to Atlanta. The boys know it, too."

The boys yelled that they were finished, saving her from saying more, or doing something stupid, something she would regret.

"See you later." He tipped his hat, pivoted and walked off the porch, a dark figure in the night. Her dog followed him.

Jenna walked back into the house, knowing that Adam wasn't a superstar, or a man who'd dated more women than Dawson had people. He was really just a cowboy who had dreamed of being a fireman.

And before long, he would be a memory.

Jenna had always dreamed of training horses. But the morning after Adam's visit, with the sun barely up, she was trying to remember why that dream had been important—especially on a morning when she would have liked to sleep late, a morning after a sleepless night.

She cinched the saddle on the gray gelding she was hoping to sell, talking to him, distracting him because he had a tendency to hold his breath and once she got the girth strap tight, he'd let his air out and the strap would be loose, causing the saddle to slide.

But she knew a few tricks, too. She moved him forward, slapped his belly and gave the strap a yank. The horse sidestepped and nodded his head a few times, his ears back to let her know that he didn't like losing.

"Oh, you poor baby." She led him to the mounting block Clint had made for her, to help her mount without the stirrups. There were challenges. Each day she faced something new, but horses she knew how to handle. She felt free when she rode, as if nothing could stop her, not even her injury.

Amputation. She could say it. Her life didn't need a man to be complete. It was complete because she was alive and she was content.

As she settled into the saddle, Jack moved a little, adjusting to the weight in the saddle. He reached back, nipping at her booted foot. She nudged his head away and urged him forward.

She rode him into the arena and from the saddle she pulled the gate closed. Jack skittered a little to the side, but she held him tight, talking to him as she edged him forward, not letting him take control.

After a few laps walking around the arena, she loosened the reins and leaned slightly. With that sign of permission, he broke into an easy lope around the arena, taking the lead with his inside front leg.

"Jack, maybe I shouldn't sell you. You really are a pretty decent guy. And decent guys are hard to find." She laughed softly because his ears twitched and went back, as if he wasn't sure if her words were an insult or compliment.

She slowed him to a walk and then stopped him with barely a flick of her wrist and the tightening of her legs. A touch of her left foot and he turned away from the pressure. She could feel his giant body rippling beneath her, beneath the saddle. He was more than a half ton of power, and yet he submitted to her control.

A truck rumbled up the drive. Jenna flicked a glance over her shoulder, expecting her brother.

It wasn't Clint.

Jack shifted, stepping a little to the right and then

backing up against the pressure of the reins. She took him around the arena again.

Adam stepped out of the truck and walked across the lawn. He looked like every other Oklahoma cowboy that she knew—faded jeans and a short-sleeved shirt buttoned up, but not tucked in. The deep red of the shirt worked with his golden tan and sandy-brown hair. This morning he wore a baseball cap, not the white cowboy hat he normally wore.

Memories of last night, of a moment when she had wanted to be held, rushed back, and so did the realization that those feelings had been hers, not his. She might not give credence to tabloids, but single at thirty-three and the number of relationships in his past did point to a possible commitment phobia on his part.

She reminded herself that she had the same phobia, because she was tired of getting left behind. And he would definitely leave her behind. He'd made that clear last night.

He stopped at the arena, leaning against the top rail of the enclosure.

"What are you doing up and around this early?" She rode Jack up to the fence. Adam ran a hand over the horse's jaw and down his neck. She glanced away, toward the house, where there was still no sign of the boys, and back to Adam. He leaned against the fence, tall and confidant.

"I thought I'd return the favor you've done me and help you out a little."

She pulled the horse back so he could step inside the enclosure. "Help me?"

"With the horses. I know you have a lot to get done this week."

"Don't you have kids showing up at your camp?"

"I do, but not until noon. Pastor Todd is going to be there in an hour. He's bringing kitchen staff to start lunch. I'll stay here a couple of hours and head that way."

"If you insist. But you won't like the job."

"I bet I won't mind."

"Could you clean the stalls? I need to work him for another fifteen minutes or so, and those stalls really need to be cleaned."

"I can clean stalls, if you have coffee."

"I keep a pot of coffee inside the tack room. I know, bad habit, but I can't help myself."

"Works for me. Pitchfork?"

Jenna smiled, because he was really going to do this. "Adam, you really don't have to do this."

"I want to."

"Fine. Pitchfork and wheelbarrow in the first stall."

He tipped his hat and nodded. "Where are the boys?"

"They'll sleep late. We stayed up and watched a movie last night."

"They're great kids. Not that I'm an expert." He didn't move away from the fence.

And Jenna couldn't untangle her thoughts from the memory of being away from the boys, worrying about them when she couldn't hold them.

"They are great. It wouldn't seem like a mom would miss much in an eight- or nine-month time period, but I missed a lot."

"You were in Iraq all that time?"

Of course he didn't know. "No, I was in rehab for nearly five months. I've only been home for five months. They were with Willow and Clint."

"I used to think I was strong." He winked and walked away, and she didn't know what to do with his statement or the way it made her feel. But he was walking away and she couldn't tell him, couldn't tell him how it felt to be so afraid, and to not feel strong at all.

The barn was stifling hot, even that early in the morning. There wasn't any breeze at all, and all of the heat got trapped inside that building beneath the metal roof. Adam pushed the wheelbarrow toward the open double doors at the end of the barn, feeling a little breeze as he got closer to the opening. He brushed his arm across his forehead and paused to watch the woman outside, pulling the saddle off the big gray horse. It was heavy and she backed up, not steady on her feet, but strong.

He knew she wouldn't want his help. He pushed the wheelbarrow out to the heap a short distance from the barn. It didn't take a genius to know that he needed to dump the old straw in that pile. He lifted the handles of the wheelbarrow and lifted, giving it a good shake and then turning it to the side to get the rest out.

Jenna walked up behind him. "You look like you could use something a little colder than coffee."

He turned, and she wrinkled her nose and smiled. "Ice water would be good. I just finished the last stall."

"You're good help. I might keep..." She laughed. "Forget that I said that."

"Yeah, I know, good help is hard to find. The boys are on the front porch."

"I saw them. They know not to come running down here when I'm working a horse. I nearly got dumped a month or so back."

"You've done all of this in a matter of months? That's pretty impressive."

"I didn't want to waste a single day getting back to life and making my dreams come true. Come on, let's get something to drink. And I have boiled eggs in the fridge if you're hungry."

"I had breakfast at The Mad Cow. Vera wanted to give me the latest on Jess and his attempts at stopping the camp. He has a lawyer, some second cousin twice removed, who is willing to help him."

"Great, that would be Kevin, and he's only doing it to help his career, which is nonexistent. But I guess this would get a guy some good publicity, trying to take down a camp owned by Adam Mackenzie."

"I guess this is one more reason for me to sell or sign the camp over to the church."

"If you think so," she said, as if she wanted to say more.

She wanted to tell him he was a quitter. She didn't need to say it, because he knew that's what she would say if she thought she could get away with it.

"Jenna, I'm not staying. And if Jess gets his way, this camp won't last. If he's doing this to get money from me, signing the camp over to the church will end that."

"I know that." She stopped and smiled up at him. "I'll miss you, that's all. And don't get that trapped look. I'm not after anything. It's just that you feel like a friend. One that I won't see again after you leave here."

"Yeah, I know." He reached for her hand. "Jenna, thank you for being the first person in a long time who doesn't want something from me."

She squeezed his hand once and let go. "You're welcome."

The boys were off the porch and running toward them, blond hair sticking up, feet bare. They wrapped their arms around Jenna and started to tell her about the mouse they'd seen the cat catch. He didn't even know that she had a cat.

"I'm going to get back to the camp. Todd will be there, and…"

She nodded. "Go ahead, I understand."

He was escaping, and she knew it. He walked away, not even understanding what he needed to escape from, or how she knew him so well, sometimes better than he seemed to know himself.

That scared him. When had anyone known him that well?

Chapter Twelve

Kids poured off the church bus as Adam parked his truck next to his trailer. They stood in groups, gangly and awkward, kids in jeans, shorts, T-shirts, with acne on their faces. The girls had short hair, the boys had long hair, they had guitars and backpacks, a few had their clothes in garbage bags.

"This is amazing." Pastor Todd walked up and stood next to him as he got out of his truck. "Wow, you could use a shower."

"I was cleaning stalls." Easy answer, but he didn't know what to say about this, about what it meant. This camp was someone else's dream. Now it was Todd's dream.

Football had been his dad's dream.

And Adam wanted to be a fireman. He smiled a little and Todd pounded him on the back, like the smile was an acknowledgment of the dream.

Adam stood back and watched, because he didn't know what to do with kids, not really. He couldn't stop his gaze from traveling down the driveway, in the direction of Jenna's. He could see the top of her blue roof from here. She knew what to do with kids.

A younger man, probably in his twenties, left the group of kids and crossed to where Adam was standing, watching.

"Adam, I'm John, the youth minister at Christian Mission. We really appreciate what you've done here, getting this together in such a short amount of time. The kids are really excited."

"I'm glad it came together for you." Adam pointed to Pastor Todd. "This is the guy who will be keeping us all on the right path. Pastor Todd from the Community Church of Dawson."

A car eased up the drive. Not just a car, it was Jess's sedan. He parked and got out. A man in a suit got out on the other side.

"Great, we don't need this."

Todd shot a glance in the direction Adam was pointing and his eyes widened. "He doesn't give up."

"No, he doesn't. He's one annoying burr under my saddle."

"He shouldn't be." Todd started in the direction of the older man. "Jess, how are you today?"

"I'd be a lot better, Pastor, if you'd give up on this crazy idea. I have my nephew here and we'd like to work out a deal with you."

"So it's all about money?" Adam joined the three men. "You know, I'm not much of a kid person, either, Mr. Lockhart, but it's just a camp. It isn't going to interfere with your life at all."

"It's a nuisance, and I have information here from county records. You didn't go through the Planning and Zoning Committee to get this place done. There are fines, laws, and permits are required."

"So you want us to send these kids home, Jess?" Pastor Todd swept a hand, indicating the kids that were being led to their dorms by workers that came with the church group. "You would really want us to do that?"

"Well, I…" Jess looked up, at the man Adam supposed was the nephew lawyer.

"We want you to go through the proper channels and get the camp approved. Which we don't think you can do. We think that it isn't in the best interest of the community, of farmers who use their land for farming, to have this camp here."

"One man with a burr under his saddle." Adam shook his head. "I'll write you a check. Tell me how much."

"Planning and Zoning, Mr. Mackenzie." The lawyer bristled.

"Right, Planning and Zoning. I need a shower, so you let me know when you decide how much you want."

Adam walked away, leaving the other men to work things out. As he walked up the steps to the trailer, he pulled out his cell phone and dialed Will.

"Adam?"

"We're going to need a lawyer."

Silence.

"What have you done?" Will's voice, a little tense. Adam smiled.

"I haven't done anything. This neighbor situation is getting crazy. He says the camp doesn't have the proper permits from Planning and Zoning. I didn't know little counties like this had Planning and Zoning." What was he thinking? This could be his way out. The county would shut the camp down. The kids would all go away. He would contact a Realtor.

"You want to save the camp?" Will's voice held a hint of laughter Adam didn't appreciate.

"I don't care about the camp." He looked out the

window at kids running around the dorm, and two boys playing catch. "The people around here want the camp."

"Right. Okay, you're the hard-hearted football player who doesn't care. The community cares. Gotcha. I'll make sure no one ever knows your secret."

"Thanks, I'm sure you'll do that. So, contact a lawyer, see what we need to do with this county situation, and with Jess Lockhart. He says it is about zoning, but I have a feeling it's about a check. I think if I'd paid him off to start, it never would have gone to the county officials."

"So you called his bluff and now he's stuck being the bad guy taking down Camp Hope."

"Yeah, he's the bad guy." Adam stood at the door and watched the old guy in bib overalls get in his car. Not exactly the picture of the villain.

"I'll get on this. But I really think Billy got the permit."

"Then we need to get that information. Or find out who he talked to on that committee."

"I'll take care of it." Will sounded confidant. Adam was glad, because he felt more like someone about to write another big check.

Adam slipped the phone back into his pocket and closed his eyes. For a long time he'd been too busy for God. And then he'd thought he was too strong to need God.

And now, he wasn't busy or strong. He was wandering in a desert, wondering if there was a clear way out, or any real answers.

Jenna pulled up to the camp as kids filed out of the dorms and down to the chapel. Next to her, Timmy and David unbuckled their seat belts.

"Stay with me, guys. I know they have activities for you, but until we know what and with whom, you're not going to take off. Understood?"

Twin looks of wide-eyed surprise and disappointment. "Okay."

She got out of her truck and the boys each grabbed a hand. Sometimes they swung too hard, knocking her off balance. But she didn't want their lives to be about the words *Be careful with Mom*.

As she walked up the steps to the cafeteria, she heard the door of the trailer close. Glancing back, she watched as Adam took the steps two at a time, and she knew that he was in his own world, not aware of what was going on around him.

She stepped through the doors of the kitchen and the boys let go of her hands and ran to Pastor Todd's wife, Lori.

"Jenna, I can take them with me. We're going to eat lunch and then I have little projects for the children of the camp workers." Lori had hold of the boys.

Jenna eyed her offspring. "You boys go with Miss Lori, and make sure you do what she says."

And then they were gone. She walked behind the stainless-steel serving counter where Louisa and several others were fixing the last pile of sandwiches.

"I'm here to work."

"That's great, honey. Why don't you help us serve sandwiches." Louisa handed her a pair of gloves. "How you feelin' today, Jenna?"

"Good." She slipped the gloves on as the door opened. It wasn't the campers. Adam paused in the doorway and then closed the door behind him.

She had been right; he looked like it had been a long day. Maybe cleaning stalls was too much for him. She smiled at the thought. She'd like for something to get the better of him.

"Jenna." He walked back to the sink to wash his hands. "Get all of your work finished?"

"Yes, thanks to you." And she shouldn't have said that, because a half-dozen pairs of eyes turned in their direction.

He stepped into place next to her behind the serving counter and pulled on the latex gloves that Louisa handed him. Jenna tried to ignore him, but he was grinning as he leaned closer.

"Bet you wish you wouldn't have said that out loud."

"I kind of do wish that," she whispered back, keeping her focus on the door that the teens were about to plow through.

"You're cute when you're beet-red. But don't worry, I don't think anyone else has noticed."

She glanced up at him. "Thanks, cowboy, you're such an encourager."

"I do my best." He nudged her a little with his shoulder. But then the door opened and the moment ended as a line of hungry teenagers swarmed the kitchen like ants on a honey trail. Or so Louisa said.

Jenna dropped a sandwich on the tray that one of the teens slid in front of her. She smiled at the girl, thinking about those years, how it had felt to be that young, that worried about the future and what people thought about her.

And now, she had other worries, but she knew who her friends were. She knew not to worry about things like being a part of a crowd that didn't really care about her.

She knew now that real friends mattered, and if she had to work at earning a friendship, acting like someone she wasn't to impress somebody, it wasn't friendship.

"How you feeling?" Adam's voice took her from that moment of looking back.

"I'm good. Why do you ask?"

His hand slid behind her back. "I'm asking because I really don't want you to wear yourself out. I've been doing research and..."

"Oh, no. You have?" She cycled through a flash of emotions and landed on the one overwhelming truth—it was really very sweet. The shy expression on his face made her want to cup his cheeks in her hands and kiss him. What a mess. "You're a good man, Adam Mackenzie."

"Well, I can't say that anyone has ever called me that."

"Then they should have. I'm going to finish up here and then help with crafts. What about you?"

He dropped chips on the tray of the young man who had just come through the door. There were more outside, still being herded in by camp counselors.

"What do you mean, what about me?"

"Are you going to help with anything this afternoon?"

"I hadn't planned on it." He kept a steady action of placing bags of chips on the trays of the young people walking through the line. "I don't even know if I'm qualified to serve meals let alone do other things."

"You're doing a great job."

A break in kids gave them privacy. He turned to face her, pulling on the latex gloves that were tighter on his hand than on hers.

"I'm pretending. Jenna, I'm not the guy who works with teens or runs a camp. When I look in your eyes, I can see that you want me to be that person. I'm not."

More kids filed through the line.

"I'm not trying to push you." She put the last sandwich on the tray of the last kid.

He pulled off his gloves and tossed them into the trash. "Yes, you are. Since I showed up in Dawson, people have had plans for me. I could really do without that for a while."

"What does that mean?" She followed him out the door of the kitchen. He had been walking fast, but he slowed for her, holding his hand out as she approached the steps.

She took his hand and eased down the steps, easing because of the pain, and feeling less than confident. "So?"

He kept hold of her hand. "Jenna, I played football because it's what I'm good at, and because I didn't have time growing up to think about anything else. My dad, coaches, agents, they've always been there to tell me my next move. And now this camp, also not my idea, my plan."

She wanted to tell him he had everything, but maybe he didn't.

"What do you want to do? I mean, you don't have to help. There are plenty of people here. I just thought..."

"That I'd like to string some beads?"

"Help. I thought you'd like to help. There's nothing like helping a child, watching them smile and grow, to make you think..."

"About something other than myself."

She smiled up at him. "I can't tell you what to do, Adam, but at your age, maybe it is time to think about what *you* want, and where you want to be."

"Maybe it is."

Jenna let go of his hand. "I'm going to string beads, and I understand that this camp isn't what you do."

"Thank you."

Jenna walked away, and she knew that he was still standing behind her, still watching. And then she heard him running to catch up with her, and something new and unexpected sparked inside her heart.

"I thought you had other things to do?" She glanced sideways at the giant of a man walking next to her.

"I thought I did, but I checked my schedule and I'm open for the rest of the afternoon."

She touched the tips of her fingers to his. "I'm glad to hear that."

"Jenna and Adam, it's great to see the two of you. You're going to help with crafts?" Marcie Watkins handed them each a long apron. "Put this on. It'll keep you a little bit clean. Notice, I said *a little*."

"I thought we were stringing beads?" Adam leaned and whispered in her ear.

Jenna shrugged. "Me, too. Marcie, aren't we stringing beads?"

"I have choices." Marcie pulled out macaroni from a box and started setting up paint. "They can make a cross necklace with beads, or paint macaroni and string it."

"Paint macaroni?" Adam shook his head. "Sounds like fun."

"It will be fun. Stop being a scrooge."

Jenna slipped the apron over her head and then pulled it to tie behind her back. As she pulled the ends tight, she watched Adam trying to get his straight, fussing with the tie behind his back. Awkward didn't begin to describe it.

"Can I help?"

"Probably." He turned so she could tie the apron.

When he turned around she laughed. He was a giant in a paper bib and a cowboy hat.

"Okay, this is funny, but here come the kids." Marcie was in the middle of her little group of helpers, four of them in aprons. "Today they can either make a cross with beads—Julie will help with that—or they can paint the macaroni. We'll let the kids string the macaroni tomorrow. We'll have a station for painting red, green, white, black. Got it, everyone?"

"What if a kid wants blue?" Adam mumbled as Marcie stationed him in front of the red paint. A tub of paint, four plates, four brushes and wipes to clean their hands. "What teenager is going to want to do this?"

"You'd be surprised. Kids like simple things. Adults always believe that only complicated things can make a kid happy." Jenna poured paint into the pan on the table in front of her. "Besides, there are kids as young as ten in this group."

"Oh." He looked around them, distracted. "You need to sit down."

"I don't." But she really did.

He was already moving away from her, toward chairs stacked in the chapel. He grabbed one off the pile and walked back with it, putting it behind her.

"There, does that work?"

She sat down, nodding. "It works. Thank you."

"Okay, now, why can't the kids have blue?"

She laughed. "You really do have a one-track mind. Black for sin, red for the shed blood of Jesus, white for sins washed away, green for peace or love, I always get that one confused."

"Got it. No blue."

"No blue." She reached up, letting her fingers slide through his for a moment, not wanting to think about how it felt to have this giant of a man caring about her, and caring about these kids.

Marcie slid past them, her glance on their intertwined fingers, and she looked away, because Marcie didn't gossip. Jenna loved that about the older woman.

"Mr. Mackenzie, the kids will be at your station first." But there was an edge to her voice. A protective, mother-hen edge.

Adam moved, breaking the connection between their

hands. And Jenna didn't blame him. It had been a silly high school thing to do, reaching for his hand that way. She thought about her heart, broken one too many times, and the boys, because they thought he was a hero.

None of them needed to go through this, through moving forward, getting over a silly summer fling.

Chapter Thirteen

The group of kids lined up in front of the macaroni-painting station, and Adam thought it looked like a lot more than ten. But after counting, he realized it really was just ten.

"Can we eat this?" one boy asked, his smile crooked and his eyes full of humor. His T-shirt was too big and his jeans a little too short.

"No, this shouldn't be eaten. It isn't cooked. We're just painting it." Adam handed the boy a brush.

"I was joking, man. Don't get so uptight."

Uptight? Was he really? He shrugged a few times, thinking that might loosen him up. Nope, still uptight. The boy shook his head and laughed. "Dude, you gotta lighten up."

"Young man, that is not a dude. That is Mr. Mackenzie and you need to learn some manners." Marcie slipped in between them, a powerhouse of a woman with gray hair and glasses. She stared the boy down, and still managed to look loving. "While we're here, we won't say *dude*. Understood?"

"Yes, ma'am." The boy lost his mirth, lost his swagger. Marcie could put a pro coach to shame.

"Hey, partner, it's okay." Adam smiled because he'd almost said *dude*.

"Mr. Mackenzie, do you think we could shoot some hoops?" The boy nodded to the basketball court fifty feet away and the ball, still lying in the grass.

"We might manage to do that, if it fits into the schedule."

"You'd play with us?" the boy continued.

"Sure I would." Adam swallowed against the painful tightening in his throat. "What's your name?"

"Chuck." The boy painted his macaroni. "This is cool. I like the red the best. I'm going to be a preacher someday."

"That's great, Chuck." Adam loosened up, and it was easy with a kid like that smiling at him. It wasn't about his autograph or football; it was about this camp. And the kid was the hero.

He wasn't a kid person, had never been the guy on the team that signed up for children's charity events. Now he wondered why.

"Come on, move on over to Jenna's station, kids. We need to get this moving along." Marcie clapped, but her smile was big and Adam knew she loved the kids, every single one of them.

He watched as they painted and she walked behind them, talking to them, hugging them, sharing stories about herself and the days when she'd been young enough to paint macaroni necklaces. One boy asked her if he had to wear it. She told him that he didn't have to, but he could give it to someone, to a younger child and tell them what he'd learned. She hoped they would all go home and tell what they'd learned to younger children who couldn't attend.

"Why aren't there younger kids here?" Adam whispered to Jenna.

She stood and poured more paint into her container. "They don't want to get kids too young in here with the teens. I think this group ranges in ages from ten to fourteen. They have a senior high class they'd like to bring later."

"Oh." Adam handed a younger girl a few wipes to clean her messy hands. "Wipe them up good, so you don't ruin your clothes."

She looked down at her knee-length shorts and T-shirt and then smiled up at him. "It's okay. I don't think I can hurt these."

The hole in his heart grew. He'd never gone without, not once in his life. He wondered how many of these kids went without decent meals, or woke up cold in the winter. He knew that it happened, but facing it, seeing it for himself, was shifting the part of his life that had been all about him.

This had changed Billy. He had seen kids like these and wanted to do something about it. He had just gotten sidetracked along the way. Billy had had a good heart.

"More paint." Jenna sat back down, but she nodded toward his paint. It was nearly empty and three children remained. A girl with a thin face and long brown hair moved up to the table. Her clothes were threadbare and her smile was weak. Her hands shook when she reached for the brush.

"Are you okay?" Adam lowered his voice, so it didn't boom and scare her to death.

She looked up, big gray eyes averted, not looking at him. She nodded but he didn't believe a kid could look like that, with a face that pale, and be okay. He glanced down at Jenna. She was already on her feet.

"Honey, can I do something for you?"

The child shook her head. The paintbrush was in her hand and she swiped red over her macaroni. She sniffled and wiped at her nose and eyes with her arm.

Where was Marcie? Adam looked behind him. She had just been there, but she mentioned cleaning supplies for when they finished. Jenna stood and started around the table.

"Let me help. Are you hungry?"

The girl nodded.

"Didn't you get lunch?" Jenna asked, her voice tender, gentle.

The girl shook her head. Chuck, at the end of the painting table, came back to them, his freckled little face a mask of seriousness. Adam really liked that kid.

"She didn't get any lunch 'cause that bully, Danny, took her sandwich and chips. She just got milk."

"Well, now, that isn't going to work." Adam knew his voice probably rattled the poles that held up the tent. The girl cowered against Jenna, her gray eyes wide.

"Calm down, Goliath." Jenna's lips pursed and she scrunched her nose at him.

The girl giggled a little. "He does kind of look like Goliath."

"Yeah, well, we can take him down with a single stone and a little faith, so we won't worry about him. He's just loud and doesn't know any better."

"We need to get her some lunch and have a talk with Danny." Adam kept his voice a little quieter, and he hoped a little less frightening.

"We'll do that. But how about if we let Pastor Todd or John talk to Danny." Jenna winked at the girl and then smiled a silly smile at him. With her arm around the girl, she moved away from the tent. "We'll go see if we can get her something to eat."

"Okay." And leave him with the kids? He did have another helper or two, but they'd kept pretty quiet at their end of the table, casting curious glances his way, but not speaking.

"Can we still play basketball?" Chuck, not about to give up.

"Yeah, we can play."

"Cool. I'm going to play basketball with Adam Mackenzie."

Adam laughed, because he couldn't believe that was all it took for this kid. He glanced behind him, watching as Jenna walked across the lawn with the little girl. And he wondered who Danny was that he'd take food from another child.

Jenna watched the little girl Cara eat the sandwich and chips that they'd found with the leftovers in the fridge. The child barely chewed the food and then she licked her fingers, not caring that she was being watched. When she finished she wiped her hands and looked up.

"That was good." Cara smiled again, the gesture transforming her pixie face. "Can I go play now?"

"You can. I think it's free time for an hour or so." Jenna nearly fell over with the force of Cara's hug. And then the girl was out the door and running across the lawn.

Slower than earlier in the day, Jenna walked out the door and watched as Adam shot the basketball, making it into the basket and then catching it, tossing it to Chuck. The boy aimed, but the ball hit the rim of the net and bounced away. He ran after it and when he returned, Adam stood next to him, showing him how to throw, how to make the shot.

He was a hero. Her boys had seen that in him from the beginning. He knew how to stop, how to just give what the kids needed. And he didn't even know that about himself. He didn't know that part of Adam Mackenzie that made people feel good.

Jenna sat down on the bench a short distance from the court. Timmy and David ran out of the back part of the kitchen where there were classrooms. They were carrying crosses made from sticks and yarn.

"You guys ready to go?"

"Do we have to?" Timmy hugged her tight and she leaned back, sitting hard on the bench that she'd vacated. He plopped down next to her. "We like the camp."

"I know you do, but the camp is for older kids. You got to come today because I was working. And now we need to go home, clean house and feed the horses."

"Couldn't Uncle Clint feed?" David sat down next to her, his curious gaze lingering on her face, because he was always the one who noticed. "We could watch a movie together."

"No, Uncle Clint can't feed. He took a load of bulls to Tulsa today. We'll be fine together. Come on, guys, cheer up."

"We'll get to come back?" Timmy asked as he stood and reached for her hand, thinking he was big enough to pull her to her feet. He did a pretty good job of it.

"Yeah, we'll come back." She followed them across the lawn, past the trailer that Adam lived in, and past the row of cars the workers had parked next to it. Her truck was at the end of that line of cars.

Today it was a really long walk.

"Hey, where are you going?" Adam's voice, and she could hear his feet pounding the ground. She turned and he was running after them, his long legs in shorts, no jeans this time.

"I'm taking the boys home. They're exhausted."

She was exhausted. "And I need to get things caught up at home."

"Do you need help?"

"Of course I don't." Her eyes stung with tears she wouldn't let fall, because maybe she was the only person that got it, that he was this kind. The boys ran on to the truck and she let them go.

Adam stood next to her. "Jenna, I can feed the horses. Let me change and I'll even drive you home. I can walk back."

"Adam, really…"

"You can stop arguing."

She closed her eyes and nodded. "I can stop arguing. But it isn't time for them to be fed."

He smiled. "Okay, then I'll come over later?"

"We'll see. You know, I really can do this myself. I'm used to it. I'll go home, rest a little, and be back at it."

A car door slammed. She glanced behind her, and Adam groaned a little. "My dad."

"Really?" She watched the older gentleman as he walked toward them, his smile a little hesitant.

"Dad." Adam held out a hand to his father, and Pastor Mackenzie took it, holding it tight for a minute.

"I came here to help you work. I'd like to see this camp that Billy couldn't stop talking about. You never know, our church might want to help out."

"I'll give you a tour." Adam looked trapped, and Jenna backed away, giving what she hoped was a clear signal that she didn't need him and he should spend time with his dad.

"I'll see you tomorrow." Jenna touched Adam's arm briefly. "Mr. Mackenzie, it was good meeting you."

Adam rubbed his forehead. "I'm sorry. Jenna Cameron, this is my dad, Jerry Mackenzie."

"Good to meet you, Jenna."

"The boys." Jenna nodded in the direction of the truck. "I need to go before they start it and drive themselves home."

"I'll talk to you later." Adam winked. "Not tomorrow."

"Well, she seems like a nice girl." Adam's dad stood next to him, watching the truck pull down the drive.

"She's a mom, not a girl." Adam let out a deep breath and relaxed. "I didn't expect to see you here today."

"I know you didn't, but I told your mother that I'd like to see what's kept you here."

Adam bristled a little under that comment. "You didn't expect me to stay?"

"Did you expect to stay?"

Adam stopped walking. He stared out over the camp, quiet in the late-afternoon heat. The kids were in the chapel behind the door, doing skits. Everything was neat and clean. It looked like a camp—not a summer camp like the ones attended by the children of his friends, with pools, tennis and gymnasiums, but a good camp where kids could have fun for a week.

And he hadn't planned to stay. He had wanted to sell it as soon as possible. Until just a few days ago he had wanted Jess Lockhart to get his way and shut it down.

A couple of weeks and his life had changed.

"No, Dad, you're right. I hadn't planned on staying. At least not staying for this reason, to get it up and running."

"Maybe this is your fire?"

Adam shook his head, not getting it. "My fire."

"You wanted to be a fireman. Remember, even when you were little, you begged me to take you to town so you could ride on the fire truck."

"Yeah, I remember." He had forgotten, but now it came back to him, that moment on the front seat of that truck, flipping switches that sounded sirens. He had always wanted to be a fireman.

But this wasn't his fire. Unless a fire was just an emergency that needed to be put out. He could admit that the place meant something to him, something more than he had planned. But it would feel good to turn it over to Pastor Todd, knowing it would continue.

"Are you still planning the job in Atlanta, then?" Jerry Mackenzie stopped a short distance from the chapel. It was a big building with screened sides, a roof and a tall steeple. Ceiling fans circulated the air, adding a little breeze to cool the kids sitting on the wooden pews.

Adam watched as four kids on the stage worked together to create a skit. He smiled at their seriousness. And he remembered church camp when he was ten, and how he had felt about his faith.

"Yeah, I'm still leaving." And it wouldn't be as easy as he had once thought. He had found a group of people that were as willing to be used as he was unwilling to be used. Two weeks had changed his life.

"Let's look at what else you have here. I don't want to interrupt the kids."

But for a minute they stood watching the kids who were talking now, saying the words to "Amazing Grace," and acting it out. Adam smiled as one child wandered around on the stage and another went to help him find his way to a child who was playing Jesus: "was lost, but now he's found."

"Let's go." Adam walked away, hurting on the inside, because he felt like he'd been lost for a long time and now that he was found, he was going to leave again.

* * *

After dinner, Adam watched his dad drive away, and then he started down the drive on foot, in the direction of Jenna's. He wanted to check on her. He also wanted to walk and think. Maybe even pray.

As he walked up her drive, the dog ran to greet him.

"Dog, you really need a name. I can't believe that someone as emotional as Jenna Cameron left you with a moniker like that."

He walked past the house to the barn. He could see her inside, sitting at the table with the boys. They had their heads bowed. His heart did a strange clench. He'd have to tell them goodbye.

And it wasn't going to be easy.

Now he understood why Jenna hadn't wanted the boys to get attached. But at least they were prepared. He hadn't been prepared for the thoughts of missing her, missing them, that assailed him. He had never expected it to be hard to leave.

The dog nudged his leg. He looked down and the animal pushed him again with the stick it had picked up. Adam took the stick and tossed it and then he walked through the double doors of the barn, taking a second to adjust to the dark, and to the smell of animals, hay and dust.

From outside in the corral, horses whinnied to him, not caring that it wasn't Jenna. They just wanted their evening meal. He opened the door to the feed room and flipped on the light. A bare bulb hanging from the ceiling flashed on, bright in the dark, windowless interior. A mouse ran behind the covered barrel that held the grain and something rustled in the empty feed sacks.

He grabbed a bucket, pulled off the lid of the barrel and scooped out grain. Three scoops for the two horses in the corral. She had fed the horses in the field that morning. So the two in the corral needed grain and hay. He couldn't forget water. In the late-June heat, that was easy to remember.

He walked outside, back into bright sunlight. The horses trotted over and he poured the feed in the trough, half on one end, half on the other. Not that it mattered, because the two animals went back and forth, ears back, the dominant horse, a big bay, eating at one pile and then chasing the black-and-white paint away from the other pile.

The dog barked, like he knew and wanted to do something about it. "Buddy, you're going to have to let them work it out."

The dog wagged his tail. "Yeah, Buddy. That's your name."

The dog wasn't his.

The dog looked up at him, sitting back and wagging his tail. "Yeah, you did good. Come on, let's drag the hose out here and fill up the water."

A car rolled up the drive, drawing the dog's attention away from farm work. The animal sat at the gate and barked. Adam turned on the hose and stuck it in the tank and then he walked out the gate to greet Pastor Todd.

"Jenna's in the house," Adam explained as he met the other man at the front of the barn.

"I know, but I'm here to see you. Jess called me."

"Great. What now?"

"He finally came clean."

Adam lifted his hat, ran a hand through his hair and settled the hat back in place, pushing it down a little tighter.

"He has demands? What is up with this guy?"

"He wants to sell you the twenty-acre field that sits between your place and his."

"I don't want his twenty acres." Adam turned and walked back to the barn. "You can come with me. I have another water tank to fill."

"I know you don't want the land, but I told him I'd talk to you. He gave me a fairly good price."

"I don't want his land." Adam turned, shaking his head. He grabbed the hose and walked the short distance to the tank that watered the horses in the field. "I'm not going to have this old guy extort money from me. If I buy this land then he'll have another problem, something else he wants from me."

"I don't think so. I think he's looking for a way out of town. This was his wife's hometown and he wants to go back to Nebraska."

"Let him go." Adam reached to scratch the jaw of the gray gelding that came up to the fence to drink. The horse pushed against his hand and then moved away, sticking his nose into the fresh water and swishing it before taking a long drink.

"Adam, he's going to a meeting tomorrow, taking his lawyer. They're going to try and find a loophole that takes away your right to have this camp."

Adam rubbed his brow and thought about it, about the camp, about the church and the kids. It was all on him.

The one guy who didn't even want to be here had to make the tough decisions for this camp that he'd never planned to have anything to do with. A short month ago he'd been living his life in Atlanta, clubbing on weekends, dating a model who had only one name, and never knowing who he could trust.

That part of the equation had been left out of the biography of his life. When magazines wrote about him, it was about the nightlife, the women, the money and the rumors.

It was never about loneliness.

"Give me time." Adam sighed, because maybe they didn't have time. They had another group of kids coming in two weeks. The camp had, not him. "I have lawyers working on this."

"I'm sorry, I don't want to push you into something you don't want to do. I wanted to present the facts, and then the decision is up to you."

"I'll take that into consideration." He smiled at Todd. "I'll even pray. But let me see what my lawyer comes up with. You know, this is something Billy should have taken care of, this zoning problem. And there's a chance he did take care of it."

"Or he saw something he could do and he went forward, not realizing how much trouble it could cause."

"Yeah, he had a habit of doing that." Good-hearted or not.

"Well, I'm going to head out. They're having a song service at the camp and then roasting marshmallows."

"Sounds like a good time." Adam liked the idea of roasting marshmallows. He hadn't done that in years. "I'll be over to join them after I check on Jenna and the boys."

"I think the kids at the camp would love it if you joined them."

Adam nodded and watched as a guy that felt a lot like a friend walked away. When he walked back to the corral, the water was running over. Adam pulled the hose out and walked back to the barn to turn off the spigot. When he walked out of the barn, the boys were waiting for him.

"We had pizza for supper," Timmy said. "It's the frozen kind, but it's good. We have leftovers if you want some."

"That's great, guys." Adam walked toward the house, the boys at his side.

"Mom said you can have ice cream, too."

"Did she?" He grinned down at them. They were running around him, full of energy, the dog chasing, barking. He couldn't help but think about the quiet days, when he'd only had himself and his team to think about.

"Yep, she did. She said, 'If he wants to eat, he can, Timmy, but you can't make him.' And I said we could, probably."

Adam laughed at the little mimic and reached down to rub the kid's blond head. "Timmy, you crack me up."

"Yeah, my mom said that, too."

"I thought you might like the kind of pizza with everything." David grinned up at him. "That's the kind that grown-ups who eat onions like."

"Yep, I must be a grown-up."

"Do you know that my mom's leg has a sore on it?" David looked down, kicking at a rock and then walking on. "She might need a doctor if that keeps up."

David, repeating Jenna, the way Timmy usually did. "I'll check on her, okay?"

"That would be good, because she doesn't want Uncle Clint to worry." David ran on ahead of him, into the house. Timmy looked up, like the little man of the house, taking things more seriously than people thought, Adam guessed.

"We think she needs to rest."

"I think she probably does, too," Adam agreed. He reached and Timmy took his hand. And possibly his heart, if that's what it felt like to lose a guy's heart to a kid, to a family. Like a squeeze, netting his emotions, making him rethink everything.

It took him a minute to shake himself loose from that feeling, to remind himself that he wasn't what Jenna or these kids needed. But for that minute he wanted to be the one who took care of them.

Jenna and the boys needed someone who didn't have doubts, a guy that knew how to keep his life together, a man who knew how to be from Oklahoma.

Not him.

Chapter Fourteen

Jenna opened the front door, offering a smile to a guy that looked pretty cornered. The boys had done that to him, the way she knew they would. Because they thought he was it. And she didn't know how to explain that he was a friend who would only be a friend for a season. Life brought people who stayed forever and people who stayed for a short time.

She knew that. Her boys had other plans. They wanted him to coach their little league, teach them to play football and go with them to the lake because they thought he lived at the camp. Jenna wanted to cry because she hurt all the way to her heart.

"I heard that you have pizza." He walked up the steps.

She nodded and motioned him inside. "I do."

"The boys invited me."

"I told them they could." She started toward the kitchen, knowing he'd follow. "I had a salad. You go ahead and help yourself. I need to take care of something while you guys eat."

He looked down, blue eyes studying her face, and then he nodded. "Let me know if you need anything."

"I'm good."

But she wasn't. She walked into her room and sat down on the edge of her bed, wanting to cry. She buried her face in her hands, fighting back the tears, fighting to be strong.

For a long time she didn't move, just enjoyed not having to stand up. Finally she did what she needed to do—took off the prosthesis and then the socks that kept it in place.

Outside her room she could hear David and Timmy telling Adam why they liked the cartoon on TV, and he agreed, laughing when they said he was as strong as that hero, and probably faster. She used to be their hero, the person who was able to climb trees to save kittens, show them how to jump rope and run around bases.

Now she felt weak, and not at all like the woman who should have Adam Mackenzie sitting in her living room. She smiled a little at that, because she knew that her life would be a story for the media that liked to report on his life. And her life wasn't a story at all. She was a mom making the best of the hand that she'd been dealt. And she was more than a survivor. Surviving sounded more like someone getting by, hanging on, and she planned on doing more than that.

She wasn't going to sit in a dark bedroom, hiding in shame.

She had nothing to be ashamed of.

She grabbed the crutches and stood. When she walked into the living room, the three guys turned and smiled at her, but then went back to their cartoon. As if this was a normal night and she hadn't just tripped over the rug. She loved them for that. Loved her boys.

Her gaze shifted from the two tiny faces of her twins to the other face, now familiar to her. He was a friend. Nothing more.

"Did you have ice cream?"

Adam nodded, but kept watching the cartoon.

"Okay, I'm going to have some. You guys have fun."

"I am." He hugged the boys close and stood to follow her. She knew without looking because the boys groaned and then told Adam she really didn't need his help. He told them he knew that, but he thought he'd keep her company.

She was scooping out butter pecan when he walked through the door. "I really don't need help, you know."

"I know. But you do look exhausted."

"Thank you, that's what every woman wants to hear." She set the timer for thirty seconds before turning to face him, leaning a little against the counter. "Truth is I am exhausted. Walking with a prosthesis takes more energy per step than walking with two good legs. Some days it wears me out. But I am better. In the beginning I could make it for a few hours and had to give up. Now I can get through a good day, sometimes a long day. I'm not up to long trips to the mall or five-mile hikes, but I'll get there."

"I think you will, too. I think you'll climb mountains."

He watched as she poured tea into a thermal cup and snapped the lid into place. She could eat standing up, and then carry the mug without spilling it. Adam reached for the bowl of ice cream.

"I can carry this for you."

"Thank you." Heat started up her neck into her cheeks. "I'm going to sit at the table."

He set the bowl down.

"Todd says that Jess wants to sell me some land."

Jenna nodded and sat down. He sat across from her. "That sounds about right. I think he had a lot of medical bills when he lost his wife."

"So the camp is bad, a blight on the community, unless I give him money."

She smiled. "Adam, he's hurting."

"You think I should give him the money?"

"I can't tell you how to handle this."

"I don't know. I'll see what my lawyer comes back with."

"It'll work out." She looked up. "When are you leaving?"

That night her boys had prayed for him when they blessed the food, asking God to keep him at the camp. Afterward she'd explained that Adam had to do what he was supposed to do and they had to accept the fact that he was leaving.

"Soon, I guess. I promised my family I would come over for lunch this Sunday. I'm still waiting for Will to finalize the date for my interview." He twiddled his thumbs and didn't look at her. "The church that's here now, they want to bring older teens in two weeks, if we can pull it off. Todd thinks it can be done."

"I think it can. And about that job, they're going to want you to work for them. I know you'll get it."

"I don't know. They had a problem a year or so back with one of their guys having some personal issues. They're a little more cautious these days."

"And their issue with you is what?" She should have stopped herself from asking that question, but curiosity got to her.

"My partying ways. My so-called rough edges. I have a lot of them, you know? I've been fined for fighting with refs—back in the old days, of course. I've fought with reporters." He smiled but it didn't quite reach his eyes. "A few years ago I had some problems with a woman. She tried to claim we were married. We weren't. She claimed that one of her boys was mine. He wasn't. She put him through—" He looked up. "She put him through a lot. He was eight. I had only known her for three months."

"What did she want from you?"

"Money and a dad for her kid."

Jenna stood up, not sure what to say or if she should defend herself. She didn't need a father for her boys. She wasn't looking for someone to fill that role in her life. Definitely not an unwilling someone. More important, she didn't want her boys to think of him like that, because she didn't want them to be hurt.

All of those thoughts rolled through her mind, but she didn't say any of it. She walked out and into the living room, where the boys were dozing off on the sofa. They'd had a long day. The room was dark and the air conditioner was working hard to keep the heat out of the room.

To keep from waking them, she walked outside. Adam followed her, closing the door behind them. He stood behind her at the edge of the porch.

"I don't think that you're like Morgan." He spoke softly. "I know that you aren't. You're strong and independent. Maybe a little too independent. Your boys have you. They have Clint and Willow. They have this community."

She nodded. Yes, the boys had all of those people. And so did she. So why did she feel so lonely with Adam standing behind her, not touching her? Why in the world did her heart feel as if it was yearning for something she had marked out of her life, out of her future, left off her list? She didn't need more rejection, more goodbyes. Or worse, someone walking away without looking back.

And her heart ached because she wanted him to touch her, to reach out and hold her, even as her smart self was telling her to say goodbye and walk away before he did.

Her smart self was so not in control of this situation.

She turned, and when she did, he wrapped an arm around her and took the crutches. He leaned them against the wall of the house. "You don't need those. I'm here."

His words were soft, whispered against her cheek. His arms were around her, holding her close, and she held on to his upper arms, solid muscle, strong. Strong enough for both of them.

When his lips touched hers, she heard him sigh, felt his chest heave, and she reciprocated, because there was something so sweet, so gentle in his touch, in that moment when their lips met. Her heart felt like it had finally grabbed hold of what it had been seeking.

She held on to him, leaning into his strength, and his lips grazed her cheek, rubbing lightly. His hands remained on her back, holding her tight.

"You're beautiful." His whispered words brought her back to reality.

"Stop." She moved away, but his lips followed, claiming hers again.

"You're beautiful." He whispered it again, near her ear, his cheek brushing hers.

She hopped to her crutches and leaned against the side of the house. "You can say that because this is easy for you. You're going back to Atlanta. I'm staying here in Oklahoma. This will be a memory for you. But this is my reality. This is my life."

"Jenna, I'm sorry. I thought we both…"

"Wanted to be kissed, to be held. Yes, we did. But don't complicate this. Don't make it about us. I'm a mom, Adam. This is about more than me and you, and a sweet moment on a summer night. It's about two little boys. It's about what happens tomorrow."

"I know." He closed the distance between them and

his arms slipped around her waist, holding her close. "I know, and I think I've just taken advantage of what felt like a great friendship."

"I think we've both messed up." She didn't move from his embrace, because it felt good in his arms. But she was coming to her senses, remembering why romance wasn't a part of her five-year plan. "I had my convictions, to keep you at the edge of my life so we wouldn't get hurt. The boys love you so much. And they've been walked out on too many times."

He brushed his cheek against hers and paused there. "*You've* been walked out on. Let's be honest, honey, this is about you, *your* heart, not just the boys. You need to know you really are beautiful."

She wiped away tears that rolled down her cheeks, turning away when he tried to help. "This is too much. You're too much."

"Yeah, maybe it is." He kissed her cheek. "See you tomorrow?"

Jenna shook her head. "I've made an appointment to get my prosthesis checked, or refitted. I might be out of the loop for a day or two."

"Okay. Why don't you let me stop by and feed in the morning?"

"I can do it. But thank you." She had Clint and Willow. It wouldn't be good to start relying on him, on someone who was leaving town as soon as possible.

"Jenna, you're stubborn."

"I know I am." She smiled then, and he winked as he turned and walked away, another guy who wasn't looking for reality, just a summer in Oklahoma.

Adam was sitting on his front porch the next morning, a clear view of the road, when Jenna's truck lumbered past. She was on her way to Tulsa. And he was here, with a camp full of kids. Fortunately there were people who knew what to do with those kids. He barely knew what to do with himself.

He sipped his coffee, glad for a few minutes of peace, and groaning when his cell phone rang. He picked it up, glancing at the caller ID before answering. "Hey, Will."

"Adam, I have an appointment for you. And bad news on the camp situation. I can't find anywhere at all that Billy went to Planning and Zoning. I looked at the county regulations with your lawyer, and he really feels like you did need to have a permit, some special zoning. I can get a lawyer there and have that taken care of."

"Yeah, okay, get it taken care of, and then draw up the paperwork to give this place and any funds raised on its behalf to the Dawson Community Church. Also, contact that little lawyer person that represents Jess Lockhart. Buy his twenty acres and put it in the name of Dawson Community Church."

"Got it. Here's the date of the appointment."

Adam wrote it down as Todd came up the steps. "Talk to you later, Will. And I guess I'll see you soon."

"Job interview?" Todd sat down and reached for the thermal coffeepot. "Do you have another cup?"

"Yeah, inside on the wall hook. Bring out the muffins from the bakery."

"Anything else?" Todd laughed as he walked through the door.

Adam couldn't laugh. He could only think about last night, and about packing his bags. He glanced out over the wide, open field that was his front yard, a place where he'd watched deer grazing as he drank his morning coffee two days ago.

He'd gotten used to the mobile home, to this deck, to Dawson. And now he was leaving.

"What's up?" Todd poured himself a cup of coffee and sat down. "Bad news?"

"No, good news. I have a job interview. And I'm having papers drawn up to sign this place over to you. As well as the twenty acres. I'll hire a lawyer to get the proper zoning taken care of, and we'll pay whatever fines they toss at us."

"Adam…"

"Todd, I think we're friends. This is what I want to do."

"I know, but it feels like you're cutting it loose. And I think that would have worked a week or two ago, when the camp didn't mean anything to you. But do you really want to walk away from it now?"

"I'm not walking away. I'm turning it over to someone more fit to take care of it. I'm not a camp director. I'm a football player, maybe a sports reporter or an anchorman for a network. This is your dream, and I know you're the best guy for it."

He tried to push Jenna and the boys from his mind, but it wasn't easy, especially when he saw that turtle of theirs scooting along in the weeds a short distance away.

"What about Jenna?"

Todd sipped his coffee and looked out over the camp, in the direction of the cafeteria where kids were starting to line up for breakfast.

"Jenna is great. She's been a big help."

"That's it?"

"She's a friend." Adam didn't know what else to say. He'd known her just a few weeks and she'd taught him to trust someone, and maybe to trust himself.

"Okay, she's a good person to call a friend."

"I think so."

Adam emptied the cup of coffee. "I'm going to spend the morning mowing. The grass is getting a little long."

Todd laughed. "No, it isn't, but you had that new mower delivered yesterday and like any guy, you're dying to get on it."

Adam nodded. But the truth was, he was dying to be alone and think about the fact that he was going to be leaving. And Jenna wasn't home to share that news with her. He'd watched her truck leave earlier, barely after sunrise.

And he'd be gone by sunset.

Jenna answered her phone on Wednesday afternoon, the day after her doctor's appointment, expecting it to be Clint. He'd been out of town and Willow had helped with chores.

The doctor's appointment hadn't gone the way Jenna wanted. She'd been given strict orders to rest for a few days while her prosthesis was adjusted. And she had explained that she didn't have time to rest. The doctor had asked if she had time to be hospitalized. That had seemed like the worst option, so she'd taken option B: rest.

"Hello." She stretched on the couch and reached to turn down the TV. She couldn't turn down the volume of the two boys playing upstairs. "Hey, guys, calm down."

"Jenna?"

"Adam." Missing in action. She hadn't heard from him all day yesterday.

"I'm in Atlanta."

"Oh." Her heart thudded hard against her chest. Atlanta.

"I—" he cleared his throat "— got a call that they wanted to interview me. I left yesterday. I didn't want to leave that message on your answering machine."

"Oh, okay. When are you coming back?" But her heart already knew the answer.

"I got the job, Jenna. I'm signing the camp over to the church and buying the land from Jess."

"That's good. I'll let the boys know that you had to leave." Her heart was pounding and wounded. She was so angry, so hurt. It shouldn't feel that way to say goodbye to him.

"Tell them I'm sorry I didn't get to say goodbye." He paused. "Jenna, I am sorry."

"I know, and I'll tell them." *Stoic,* she knew the word, knew how to be that person. "Adam, we knew this day would come. The boys knew you weren't staying here. But they will miss you."

"I'll miss them, too." He sighed, and she remembered too much about being in his arms. "Jenna, are you okay?"

"Of course I am."

"The doctor's appointment."

"Oh, that. Yes, well, I'm off my feet until tomorrow. Oh, someone is here. I'm glad you called."

She watched Clint's truck pull up her drive as she hung up the phone, pretending it was her idea to let Adam Mackenzie go. It felt better that way.

Clint knocked on the door. She waved them in and held her arms out for the baby. Willow handed her over and Jenna cuddled the infant close, enjoying the feel of her, and the way she smelled, like soap and lotion.

"You've been crying." Clint leaned to hug her.

"I haven't."

Willow nodded and pointed to her own eyes. "Mascara, puffy lids. I don't think it's a virus."

Jenna bit down on her bottom lip and swallowed the sob that welled up from inside.

"He's gone." Jenna sighed and said the words. "Did you know that he was gone?"

Willow nodded. "I'm sorry. We found out yesterday evening when we went to the camp chapel service."

"Jenna, you knew he'd have to go." Clint, pragmatic, brows scrunched together. "Why in the world does that bother you so much? He didn't walk out on the camp, and that's what you were worried about."

Willow punched his arm and he yelped. "You idiot, she's in love."

"I'm not in love. I'm mad because he didn't say goodbye to the boys."

"Who didn't say goodbye to us?" Timmy was standing in the door of the kitchen. "Who's gone?"

"Honey, Adam had to leave. He had a job interview and we weren't here." Jenna said it like it was expected, like it shouldn't hurt.

Timmy was shadowed by David, and both boys stared, eyes wide and welling up with tears. "He was gonna play football with us."

"Hey, guys, you still have me. I know how to play football."

The boys stared at Clint like he'd lost it. "You're not pro."

He laughed but Jenna thought he looked a little hurt. "No, I'm not pro, but I can throw a football as good as Adam Mackenzie. Why don't you guys help me with chores, okay?"

The one thing Jenna knew about Clint. He would always be there for them.

She watched as her brother took the boys out the back door, listening as they talked about their pony and the dog being called Buddy now. But Adam was gone, and he was the one that told them the dog liked that name.

Willow sat down in the chair next to the couch and she didn't say anything. Maybe because Willow knew what it was like to have that moment when a guy broke her heart. And Willow knew that a heart couldn't be glued back together with nice words.

Jenna rubbed her hands over her face and told herself she really wasn't going to cry. But tears burned her eyes and she felt the pain like a lump rising from her heart to her throat, tightening in her chest.

"I don't care about him." She took the tissue that Willow handed her. "Oh, this is ridiculous. He was a nuisance. He was never planning on staying and I knew that. And what did I do?"

"You fell in love?"

Jenna nodded. "I fell in love. And I knew that I was falling in love."

"Love. Who would have thought." Willow smiled.

"But three weeks doesn't a relationship make." Jenna uncovered her face so Willow could hear her, because Willow had reminded her by touching her arm. She needed to read lips.

"Three weeks isn't long enough to call this love," she repeated.

Willow laughed. "Right, tell that to your heart."

"My heart is obviously defective. It always picks the guys that aren't going to stay around." She gasped. "That's it. I am defective. I purposely form relationships with men who aren't dependable. That means I'm not really looking for a relationship. I'm sabotaging myself, which means…"

Willow shook her head. "Give it up. You love him. He was dependable. He was kind to you and the boys. He was gentle. Of course you fell in love with him."

"Three weeks. He'll be easy to get over." Jenna looked at her sister-in-law and sighed words she knew. "I need chocolate."

"Right. But I don't think they make enough chocolate to fix this."

And her boys. They would miss him. And she wasn't going to do this again. Next time she really would know better than to let her heart get involved.

Adam started his new job on Monday. He sat behind his new desk, in his new office, and he took phone calls. He made phone calls. He answered questions. He planned travel for the games he'd be announcing.

And he hated it.

A fist rapped on the door, short knocks, and it opened. A familiar face, blond-headed and a cheery smile. Adam leaned back and groaned. He didn't need cheering up. He didn't need optimism.

"How does it feel?" Will closed the door behind him. He stood in the center of the room, surveying the office with the dream view of Atlanta.

"It feels…" Adam leaned back in the chair and shrugged. "It feels like torture. It feels like a cage."

"Buddy, don't do this to me. This is your dream, right? This is still what you want, isn't it? Because we're still negotiating a few details on your contract and if you're going to flake out, I need to know."

"I'm not flaking."

Will sat down in the seat on the opposite side of the desk. He lifted his left leg, situating it over his right and leaning back, his arms folded behind his head. "Tell me who she is. Do we need to pay her off?"

Adam sat up, no longer amused. "That isn't funny."

Will put his foot down and leaned forward. "I know.

But sometimes it's the only way to get your attention. It's the girl from the camp."

"Woman."

"Fine, woman with two kids." Will shook his head. "As much as I wanted this for you, I really wanted it to happen here, in Atlanta. Settle down, I told you. Find some nice woman."

"I'm not thinking about settling down. We were talking about this job."

"*Torture*. I think that was the word you used."

Adam turned his chair to look out the window. He'd been doing that all morning, and comparing it to his view from the front deck of the mobile home in Dawson. He'd been thinking about Jenna driving up the road in her old truck, the two boys buckled in behind her.

Jenna Cameron was five feet of temptation that he couldn't get off his mind, because she'd taken his leaving and acted as if it didn't matter. Maybe it didn't matter.

His life was going in the direction he had planned. "This is what I want, Will. I planned this. It's one of the few things in my life that I planned for myself. I own this decision."

"Alrighty then." Will smiled big. "And you're not defensive. You've made other decisions for yourself. The camp. You made a decision to keep it going."

"Yeah, well, God might have had something to do with that."

Jenna was a distraction. He knew when he met her that she wasn't a summer romance. She was the type of woman a man married, the type he took home to meet his family. And he wasn't the type of man who married a woman like that.

She wasn't a Friday night and unreturned phone calls when things got too confining.

But man, she'd made him a better person.

"She made me feel like the kind of guy who could love a woman like her forever."

"Whoa!" Will coughed. "That's not what I thought I'd hear. I was just razzing you."

"Yeah, well, I've had nearly a week to think about the fact that I miss her more than I've ever missed anyone. I miss her boys."

"Kids. You miss kids? If you tell me you remember my daughter's name, I'm going to know that something happened to you in Oklahoma."

"Kaitlin."

Will stood up. "I'll hold off on the contract until you decide if you are positive about this job."

Positive about the job. Adam looked out the window. And he had to be positive about what he was feeling for Jenna and her kids. He couldn't go back if he didn't know for sure.

Chapter Fifteen

Jenna watched the boys play in the water hose. It was the second week of July and hotter than ever. Hotter than a flitter—whatever a flitter was. But Adam wasn't there to laugh at the joke, so it wasn't as funny.

She hadn't heard from him since he left.

The toughest part of that was that she hadn't expected to miss him so much. Two weeks of missing him shouldn't feel like two weeks separated from oxygen. The boys were laughing, spraying each other, and it wasn't about them, because they believed Adam would come back to see them.

Or maybe they were waiting for God to answer their prayers, the ones they prayed each night when they thought she wasn't listening. That Adam would be their dad. The first time she'd heard them, she'd tried to explain that for them to have a dad, she would need a husband. And she didn't want a husband. So then they'd started praying that she'd want a husband.

As much as it hurt, she smiled, because they were so sweet and she loved them so much.

"Guys, I have to feed the horses. Stay here, okay?" She walked past them and they laughed, spraying at her, but not getting close enough to hit her with the spray of water.

A car pulled up the drive. Jenna held her breath the way she always did when she heard a car, thinking it might be Adam. And it never was, and she couldn't believe she missed him this way.

It was Pastor Todd. He stopped and got out. She waited for him. He made a wide path around the boys and met her at the front of the red-painted barn. His wife had gotten out of the passenger side. She wasn't afraid of the boys and the water hose.

"What brings you out here?" She walked into the barn, enjoying that it smelled like horses, hay and grain. She had always loved this barn. Even as a child this had been her hiding place.

"I came out to tell you that we're going to do a ladies' retreat at the camp, maybe in September."

He didn't drive all the way out to her house to tell her that. She turned, giving him a look, and he blushed a little. "Really?"

"I came out to check on you." He looked into the stalls as they walked through the barn. "And to tell you that Adam called. He asked about you."

"Did he?" She pretended not to care, shrugging it off as she opened the door to the feed room. "And you told him that we're fine, right?"

She filled the bucket and walked out into the sunshine. The three horses in the corral nosed in, doing their typical chasing dance until they each settled on one of the tubs of feed.

"I told him we all miss him." He smiled as he answered.

"I guess we probably do." She stood next to Pastor Todd, watching the tank as the water level rose. The horses came up, sucking up the cool water and then playing in it, splashing with their faces in the water.

"Would you mind playing this Sunday at church?" Todd reached out and rubbed the face of the bay mare she'd bought the previous week. The horse left the water and walked up to the fence, wanting more attention.

That personality was why Jenna had bought her. She had seen the mare on the Internet and liked her eyes. It was always in the eyes—kindness or shiftiness. Even in people. She closed her eyes, remembering Adam's face, his eyes.

He had good eyes, full of light and laughter. That's what she'd seen in his interviews, that hidden part of him—maybe hidden from himself, not just from the cameras.

"Is there anything else I can do around here before I leave?" Todd pulled the water hose back and dragged it to the barn to turn it off.

"No, I'm good. Do you know the songs for Sunday?"

"Kate can give you a list. Jenna, do you love Adam Mackenzie?"

She turned, not sure how to answer, surprised that he'd ask the question. "I didn't know him long enough to love him."

"Oh, I don't know. Maybe love at first sight is really attraction or chemistry at first sight. But love, that grows from knowing someone, from the way they make us feel about ourselves—how we feel when we're with them."

Love. She blinked a few times, because her heart breaking wasn't about attraction. It was about losing someone who had changed how she felt about herself.

He had called her beautiful and she had wanted to believe that he really thought she was.

They finished feeding, turned out the lights in the barn and walked back into the bright sunlight, where the boys were playing with their trucks in the mud they'd created with the hose and Pastor Todd's wife was talking to them, complimenting their trails and hills.

"Mom, can we go see our turtle?" David pushed his truck over a pile of rocks.

"Turtle?" She stayed a safe distance from the mud puddle.

"The one at Adam's trailer. Could we go tonight and make sure he has food?"

"Not tonight, David. And he does have food. He's a turtle, and God gave them instincts so that they would know how to feed themselves."

"God gave them insects?" Timmy's nose scrunched.

"Instincts, Timmy. They know, without being told, how to eat, how to keep safe, where to go in storms."

"Sounds like a Bible lesson, doesn't it?" Pastor Todd patted her shoulder. "Turtles know when to duck into their shell, they know where to go for shelter."

Jenna groaned. "I bet we'll hear that on Sunday morning."

"You'd better believe it." He bent down and picked up a toy truck. The boys smiled up at him when he rolled it through the dirt and then parked it back on the pile of rocks. "You guys take care of your mom."

They looked up, nodding at him. They always took care of her. Even their prayers were about taking care of her. And hers were all about taking care of them.

And that's the way it should be, a mom taking care of her boys. No one was going to hurt them again. It seemed as if she'd learned that lesson more than once, but her heart kept taking chances, trying again.

She smiled at the boys. Pastor Todd was getting into the car with his wife. The dog was nipping at their tires. Timmy and David were looking up at her, as if they were waiting for an answer to a question she didn't know.

That meant they weren't giving up on the camp idea. They wanted to see the turtle. She knew what they were thinking. They probably thought Adam would be there. He wasn't. Adam was somewhere in Atlanta. He had called to check on them. But that wasn't enough. That would never feel like enough.

"Guys, we'll go see the turtle tomorrow. Tonight we're going to take it easy. We're going to have a big dinner with food from the garden and watch a movie together."

The boys didn't look as if they thought that was the best plan. She hugged them close and walked toward the house, one on each side of her. But her gaze drifted, across the road, and down. No lights shined from Camp Hope, because he was gone. He had found his dream in Atlanta.

And she was still dreaming in Oklahoma, no longer dreams of the darkness and pain, but dreams of what it had felt like in his arms. These dreams were just as painful as the nightmares they'd replaced.

Adam had driven all night, but he wasn't tired. He was wide awake, watching the sun come up over the Oklahoma horizon, turning the fields pink and gold. The horses were grazing in the field and as he poured a cup of coffee, a deer ran through the yard, right outside his kitchen window. Adam stretched and pulled his shirt down.

It was good to be home. He smiled at that thought, at how this place had become his home. This was his place. He picked up his coffee and walked outside, wondering how long it would take Jenna to find out that he was back, and what she'd say.

Maybe she'd tell him to take a hike. Or maybe she would say they could still be friends. He had a list of things he wanted to tell her about his job, about dreams and about Atlanta.

In the quiet of the morning he heard the distant roar of a truck engine coming to life. He sat down at the patio table and watched the field, the road, looking for the deer.

And then her truck came up the road, totally unexpected in the gray of early morning. He didn't stand, just waited, wondering what she was up to. She couldn't know he was here, not yet. Her truck idled up his driveway and came to a stop a short distance from the deck. She didn't get out. She sat in the truck, staring through the windshield, her eyes wide, surprised. Or maybe he imagined that look, like maybe she was glad to see him.

He stood and walked to the edge of the porch. The back door on the truck opened and the boys tumbled out, messy hair and still in their pajamas, with flip-flops on their feet. Jenna was slower getting out. She walked around the front of the truck and paused, but not the boys. They rushed him, running up the steps and tackling his legs.

"We knew you'd come back." Timmy hugged tightest. "But Mom said God didn't answer prayers that were wishes. But it was really a prayer, not a wish."

"Okay, guys, let him breathe. He's here to check on the camp and we surprised him." She looked up, a cowgirl in denim shorts, a T-shirt and canvas sneakers, her hair in a loose bun. "We came to check on the turtle. They didn't believe me that it could take care of itself. And that we probably can't find it."

She looked down, and then away from him. Her cheeks were pink and he knew that she was embarrassed.

"I haven't seen the turtle." He continued to watch her, wondering if she knew how beautiful she was, and if he told her, would she believe him.

He'd never really believed in the whole heart-in-the-throat condition, but at that moment, he knew that it existed. It was a lump that worked its way up, cutting off his air, making him want to say things that he'd never thought he'd say to anyone.

"How long are you here for?" She walked with the boys to the longer grass and he followed.

"I don't know." And he didn't. He had taken a leave of absence from a job he'd barely had a chance to start. Not a good way to start a career. "I have to be in Miami next week. But my dad's having some medical tests done and I wanted to be here."

"That's good—that you can be here." She looked away, her face in shadows. She walked a few steps, looking for the turtle. He followed her.

The boys ran ahead of them, positive the turtle wouldn't have gone far, because this was his home. As they searched, their dog came running up the road. He joined in the search, sniffing in the weeds, circling trees. The boys urged him on, like he was the greatest tracking dog in the world.

"Jenna, I'm sorry for what happened. I think we started out trying to be careful for the sake of the boys. Neither of us wanted them to be hurt, to think that there might be something…"

"Don't." She stopped and turned, her face set, not moving, not smiling. "We're grown-ups. I knew better. I knew not to let myself get involved in something that would only last a month or two. We're both too old for summer romances. Stop blaming yourself. I'm a grown woman and I made a choice. I let you into my life. I walked into yours."

"Yes, you walked into mine." He walked next to her. "And I crashed into yours."

Her mouth twitched and he knew she was fighting a smile.

"Adam, I should take the boys and go. They've been praying for you to come home. This will just confuse them."

"Confuse them?"

"They saw us kiss, and they think that means a man and woman are supposed to get married."

"Sometimes it does."

Jenna didn't know what to say. She waited, not sure of what he meant. He smiled, that soft, tender smile with a little bit of naughtiness that made him so charming.

"Yes, sometimes it does." She continued walking, away from him, from the power of his presence.

"Sometimes a kiss means I love you. Sometimes we just don't know it, not right away." He kept talking. She wanted him to stop. She wanted to tell him he couldn't walk in and out of their lives this way, with his charming wit, his cute smile, his way of making her feel like she belonged to someone.

"We have to find the turtle." She stepped through some weeds, stumbling a little when the wrong foot hit a rock. A strong hand caught her arm and held her tight.

"Careful."

"I know." She didn't mind that he didn't move his hand. They walked together in silence, not really looking for the turtle. The boys were scouring the area, talking about breakfast and bugs, and how long Adam would be in town.

"So, how long?" she asked.

"Maybe awhile."

She looked up. He paused, pulling her to a stop next to them. He pointed and she saw the turtle. Maybe their turtle, it was hard to tell.

"Guys, here it is." Adam pointed.

The twins hurried toward them, all smiles—over a turtle. She wondered if she had worn the same silly smile when she'd seen Adam on his front porch.

Timmy picked up the turtle and turned it over. "We have to see if he's ours."

Black marker on the bottom of the shell proved it was. Timmy held it up for her to look at. He'd be six in a week and reading wasn't his strongest skill, not yet. "It has more names."

"I found him before I left." Adam turned a little red, and Jenna liked that. She'd never seen him embarrassed before.

She took the turtle from Timmy. "Adam wrote his name on there with yours."

David stood on tiptoes and peeked at the shell. He smiled up at Adam. "Mom's name is on there, too."

"Yeah, I thought all of our names should be on there, because he's kind of like all of ours." Adam rested his hand on David's shoulder. "I really missed you guys."

"We missed you, but we knew you'd be back." David took the turtle. "We're going to find him some bugs to eat."

They were off and running toward the trailer. Jenna turned in that direction, taking it easy over the rough ground. Adam walked next to her, matching his pace to hers.

"Jenna, I'm not leaving." He kept walking, but she couldn't, not with an announcement like that.

"What about your job? I thought it was your dream?"

"It's still my job, but I'm going to work from here, and I only signed for six months. It'll mean traveling quite a bit." He took her hand and they kept walking. "Somewhere along the way I realized something about myself. I kept thinking about what my dreams were, and it hit me that this camp is my dream. Funny that something that started out as a thorn in my side has become the thing I dream of doing."

"You're going to run the camp?"

"And be a fireman."

She laughed and, for the first time in weeks, she felt like laughing was okay, like life was okay. "I'm glad. We need more firemen."

"I'm also going to do some dating." His fingers laced through hers. "I realized something else while I was gone—how much I missed you and the boys. I've never missed anyone before, not like this."

They walked out of the woods into the clearing next to the trailer. The boys were sitting in the grass, talking and feeding the turtle. Jenna looked up and Adam was smiling at them, the way a man smiled at people he loved.

And then he looked at her, and that look was still in his eyes, for her. He touched her cheek and then brushed his fingers through her hair, smoothing it back and then pulling it free from the bun that had kept it off her neck.

Her heart froze and then caught up with an extra few beats. He leaned and his lips touched hers, tender, strong, capturing hers in the moment, a moment she wanted to hold on to—forever.

When he moved away, she could still feel the imprint of that kiss, and his hand on her back. She kept her hands on his arms, afraid her legs weren't steady, afraid she'd already fallen further than she'd ever fallen before.

"Jenna, you're my dream, you and the boys. You're the best thing that has happened to me. You changed everything. I thought I could go back to Atlanta, carry on with my life and be fine, but I couldn't. I missed you every single day."

"I missed you, too," she whispered, because the words felt trapped somewhere near her heart. "I wanted God to hear their prayers to bring you back, because they were my prayers, too."

"He brought me back. I couldn't settle in Atlanta, not with the three of you here." He leaned, kissing her again. "I want all of our dreams to come true."

"Okay."

"So if I stay this year, we can go steady." He smiled and kissed her cheek, holding her close, his cheek brushing hers.

"And get married." She leaned into him, finally free to fall in love, because he thought she was beautiful the way she was.

And he loved her boys.

He was holding her, smiling. "Jenna, did you just propose?"

She blinked a few times, and laughed. "Yes, I guess I did. I think maybe I'm not supposed to do that."

"Then why don't you let me." He turned to find the boys. "Timmy, David, come here."

The boys scurried over, still holding their turtle. "We fed him a little bug."

"That's great. But could you guys do me a favor?"

Both boys nodded their heads and Jenna wondered what he would do. He placed the boys in front of her, and then he went down on one knee.

"You know I've had knee surgery, right?" He winked at Timmy and David. "I might not be able to get up, but that's okay. I think I'm supposed to do this from down here."

"Jenna, Timmy and David, I'd really love it if the three of you would marry me."

And the boys flew at him, knocking him back and then they were in his arms and Jenna waited, because she knew he would be holding her forever.

* * * * *

Dear Reader,

Thank you for reading the COWBOY series, and I hope you'll love *Jenna's Cowboy Hero*. If you read *A Cowboy's Heart*, you'll remember Jenna as the sister of bull rider Clint Cameron, and the mom of those two rambunctious boys, Timmy and David. She's a strong young woman who has had to overcome some difficult situations, and along the way she found faith. The one thing she has a hard time believing is that a man can love her. She no longer feels beautiful and it takes a special man to change all of that for her. It takes a man as strong as she is. I think there is a special lesson in this book: don't sell God short. Don't use the word *never*. We don't know what is around the corner, and we might find that it is exactly what we thought couldn't or wouldn't happen.

Blessings,

Brenda Minton

QUESTIONS FOR DISCUSSION

1. Adam Mackenzie feels as if he has been stuck with an unfinished camp, and used by his cousin. People have used him before. How could he change his attitude toward this situation?

2. Jenna Cameron made a five-year plan for her life. She left out relationships. Why do you think she did that?

3. Jenna is a single mom, and the twins are her first priority. What is the balance between being a mom and being a single woman?

4. Adam is determined to get the camp running, then leave. It isn't that he's a bad person, but he feels he isn't qualified to run a camp, and he hadn't planned on running it. How would you react if something like that was dumped in your lap?

5. As Adam's attitude toward the camp changes, how do you think he's changing?

6. Adam has a strained relationship with his family because of the very career that has supported him. What caused those strained relationships, especially with his father?

7. Jenna doesn't feel beautiful, but she's trying hard to feel good about herself. How do you think the amputation has changed her life?

8. Jenna is a new Christian. She grew up fighting God. Why?

9. Adam was raised in church but hasn't gone for years. Why do people like Adam walk away from church? Does it necessarily mean they've walked away from what they believe, or have they just let other things get in the way?

10. Is there a big moment that brings Adam back to his faith, or small moments that draw him back? How is that like our lives?

11. Jenna made a decision that she wouldn't fall in love, in order to protect the boys from having another man walk out on them. Can we really make those decisions to control what we feel or the things that happen in our lives?

12. How does faith play into the decisions that Jenna made, and the decisions we make for ourselves, especially if we believe that God has a plan and purpose for our lives?

13. Adam realizes that football is what he's always done, and that he never really thought about the dreams he had for his life. How connected are our dreams for our own futures and the plans that God has for us?

14. Adam reaches a point where he knows that being in Atlanta is a mistake and that his dreams are in Oklahoma with Jenna and the boys. How has he changed from who he was in the beginning of the book?

15. Jenna doesn't expect Adam to come back to Dawson, but a small part of her hopes he does. Did you think Adam would return? Why or why not?

Here is an exciting sneak preview of
TWIN TARGETS by Marta Perry,
the first book in the new 6-book
Love Inspired Suspense series
PROTECTING THE WITNESSES
available beginning January 2010

Deputy U.S. Marshal Micah McGraw forced down the sick feeling in his gut. A law enforcement professional couldn't get emotional about crime victims. He could imagine his police chief father saying the words. Or his FBI agent big brother. They wouldn't let emotion interfere with doing the job.

"Pity." The local police chief grunted.

Natural enough. The chief hadn't known Ruby Maxwell, aka Ruby Summers. He hadn't been the agent charged with relocating her to this supposedly safe environment in a small village in Montana. He didn't have to feel responsible for her death.

"This looks like a professional hit," Chief Burrows said.

"Yeah."

He knew only too well what was in the man's mind. What would a professional hit man be doing in the remote reaches of western Montana? Why would anyone want to kill this seemingly inoffensive waitress?

And most of all, what did the U.S. Marshals Service have to do with it?

All good questions. Unfortunately he couldn't answer any of them. Secrecy was the crucial element that made the Federal Witness Protection Service so successful. Breach that, and everything that had been gained in the battle against organized crime would be lost.

His cell buzzed and he turned away to answer it. "McGraw."

"You wanted the address for the woman's next of kin?" asked one of his investigators.

"Right." Ruby had a twin sister, he knew. She'd have to be notified. Since she lived back east, at least he wouldn't be the one to do that.

"Jade Summers. Librarian. Current address is 45 Rock Lane, White Rock, Montana."

For an instant Micah froze. "Are you sure of that?"

"'Course I'm sure."

After he hung up, Micah turned to stare once more at the empty shell that had been Ruby Summers. She'd made mistakes in her life, plenty of them, but she'd done the right thing in the end when she'd testified against the mob. She hadn't deserved to end up lifeless on a cold concrete floor.

As for her sister...

What exactly was an easterner like Jade Summers doing in a small town in Montana? If there was an innocent reason, he couldn't think of it.

Ruby must have tipped her off to her location. That was the only explanation, and the deed violated one of the major principles of witness protection.

Ruby had known the rules. Immediate family could be relocated with her. If they chose not to, no contact was permitted—ever.

Ruby's twin had moved to Montana. White Rock was probably forty miles or so east of Billings. Not exactly around the corner from her sister.

But the fact that she was in Montana had to mean that

they'd been in contact. And that contact just might have led to Ruby's death.

He glanced at his watch. Once his team arrived, he'd get back on the road toward Billings and beyond, to White Rock. To find Jade Summers and get some answers.

* * * * *

Will Micah get to Jade in time to
save her from a similar fate?
Find out in TWIN TARGETS,
available January 2010
from Love Inspired Suspense.

Copyright © 2010 by Harlequin Books S.A.

Love Inspired SUSPENSE

RIVETING INSPIRATIONAL ROMANCE

The witness protection program was supposed to keep Jade Summers's sister safe. So why is U.S. Marshal Micah McGraw saying her twin is dead? They soon realize the killers are really after Jade... though they don't know *why*. Finding the truth could be disastrous... but lives depend on it!

PROTECTING *the* WITNESSES

Look for

TWIN TARGETS
by **MARTA PERRY**

Available January wherever books are sold.

www.SteepleHill.com

Steeple Hill®

LIS44377

Cheyenne Rhodes has come to Redemption, Oklahoma, to start anew, not to make new friends. But single dad Trace Bowman isn't about to let her hide her heart away. He just needs to convince Cheyenne that Redemption is more than a place to hide—it's also a way to be found....

Look for

Finding Her Way Home

by

Linda Goodnight

Available January wherever books are sold.

www.SteepleHill.com

Steeple Hill®

LI87571

Love Inspired® SUSPENSE

RIVETING INSPIRATIONAL ROMANCE

The rustic lakeside homestead is supposed to be a refuge for widow Nori Edwards; however, the moment she arrives, strange and frightening things start happening. Former police officer Steve Baylor vows to protect Nori and she finally feels safe. But danger won't stay hidden forever....

Look for

WHISPER LAKE

Storm Warning

by LINDA HALL

Available January wherever books are sold.

www.SteepleHill.com

Steeple Hill®

LIS44376

LARGER-PRINT BOOKS!

**GET 2 FREE
LARGER-PRINT NOVELS
PLUS 2 FREE
MYSTERY GIFTS**

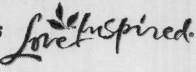

Larger-print novels are now available...

YES! Please send me 2 FREE LARGER-PRINT Love Inspired® novels and my 2 FREE mystery gifts (gifts are worth about $10). After receiving them, if I don't wish to receive any more books, I can return the shipping statement marked "cancel". If I don't cancel, I will receive 4 brand-new novels every month and be billed just $4.49 per book in the U.S. or $4.99 per book in Canada. That's a savings of over 30% off the cover price. It's quite a bargain! Shipping and handling is just 50¢ per book.* I understand that accepting the 2 free books and gifts places me under no obligation to buy anything. I can always return a shipment and cancel at any time. Even if I never buy another book, the two free books and gifts are mine to keep forever.

121 IDN EYLZ 321 IDN EYME

Name _____ (PLEASE PRINT)

Address _____ Apt. #

City _____ State/Prov. _____ Zip/Postal Code

Signature (if under 18, a parent or guardian must sign)

Mail to Steeple Hill Reader Service:

IN U.S.A.: P.O. Box 1867, Buffalo, NY 14240-1867
IN CANADA: P.O. Box 609, Fort Erie, Ontario L2A 5X3

**Are you a current subscriber of Love Inspired books
and want to receive the larger-print edition?
Call 1-800-873-8635 or visit www.morefreebooks.com.**

* Terms and prices subject to change without notice. Prices do not include applicable taxes. Sales tax applicable in N.Y. Canadian residents will be charged applicable provincial taxes and GST. Offer not valid in Quebec. This offer is limited to one order per household. All orders subject to approval. Credit or debit balances in a customer's account(s) may be offset by any other outstanding balance owed by or to the customer. Please allow 4 to 6 weeks for delivery. Offer available while quantities last.

Your Privacy: Steeple Hill Books is committed to protecting your privacy. Our Privacy Policy is available online at www.SteepleHill.com or upon request from the Reader Service. From time to time we make our lists of customers available to reputable third parties who may have a product or service of interest to you. If you would prefer we not share your name and address, please check here. ☐

LILP09

Love Inspired
HISTORICAL
INSPIRATIONAL HISTORICAL ROMANCE

Though prepared for the danger of the new frontier, Emmeline Carter didn't foresee the tornado that tore her family's wagon apart. With her family stranded and injured, there's nowhere else to turn but the fledgling Kansas settlement of High Plains, where Will Logan steps in to help. He's not cut out for family life—but Emmeline has her own ideas!

Look for

High Plains Bride

by

VALERIE HANSEN

AFTER *the* STORM
The Founding Years

Available January wherever books are sold.

www.SteepleHill.com

Steeple
Hill®

LIH82827

TITLES AVAILABLE NEXT MONTH

Available December 29, 2009

FINDING HER WAY HOME by Linda Goodnight
Redemption River

She came to Oklahoma to escape her past, but single dad Trace Bowman isn't about to let Cheyenne Rhodes hide her heart away. But will he stand by her when he learns the secret she's running from?

THE DOCTOR'S PERFECT MATCH by Irene Hannon
Lighthouse Lane

Dr. Christopher Morgan is *not* looking for love. Especially with Marci Clay. The physician and the waitress come from two very different worlds. Worlds that are about to collide in faith and love.

HER FOREVER COWBOY by Debra Clopton
Men of Mule Hollow

Mule Hollow, Texas, is chock-full of handsome cowboys. Veterinarian Susan Worth moves in, dreaming of meeting Mr. Right, who most certainly is *not* the gorgeous rescue worker blazing through town...or *is* he?

THE FAMILY NEXT DOOR by Barbara McMahon

Widower Joe Kincaid doesn't want his daughter liking their pretty new neighbor. His little girl's lost too much already. And he doesn't think the city girl will last a month in their small Maine town. But Gillian Parker isn't what he expected.

A SOLDIER'S DEVOTION by Cheryl Wyatt
Wings of Refuge

Pararescue jumper Vince Reardon doesn't want to accept Valentina Russo's heartfelt apologies for wrecking his motorcycle.... Until she shows this soldier what true devotion is really about.

MENDING FENCES by Jenna Mindel

Called home to care for her ailing mother, Laura Toivo finds herself in uncertain territory. With the help of neighbor Jack Stahl, she'll learn that life is all about connections, and that love is the greatest gift.

LICNMBPA1209